HOMING

Stephanie Domet

HOMING

Stephanie Domet

Invisible Publishing

Halifax & Toronto

Library and Archives Canada Cataloguing in Publication

Domet, Stephanie, 1970-
  Homing / Stephanie Domet.

ISBN 978-1-926743-39-4

  I. Title.

PS8607.O49H64 2013   C813'.6   C2013-901473-X

Cover design by Emily Davidson, ALL CAPS DESIGN

Typeset in Laurentian & Gibson by Megan Fildes & Robbie MacGregor
Special thanks to type designer Rod McDonald

Printed and bound in Canada

Invisible Publishing
Halifax & Toronto
www.invisiblepublishing.com

We acknowledge the support of the Canada Council for the Arts which last
year invested $20.1 million in writing and publishing throughout Canada.

Invisible Publishing recognizes the support of the Province of Nova Scotia
through the Department of Communities, Culture & Heritage. We are
pleased to work in partnership with the Culture Division to develop and
promote our cultural resources for all Nova Scotians.

NOVA SCOTIA
Communities, Culture and Heritage

Canada Council   Conseil des Arts
for the Arts   du Canada

For a few good men. For Chris Domet, who inspired it. For Ray Domet, who would have loved reading it. For Kev Corbett, who put up with me while I wrote it. And for Jeff Domet, who's always wanted to be in a book I wrote.

LEAH AWOKE TO THE COOING OF THE BIRDS. The room was dark, though slices of light crept in at the sides of the curtains. Red silk covered the cages, which were perched atop the bookcase. From beneath the fabric, she heard the ruffling of feathers and the soft, guttural cries of the mourning doves. Get up, she imagined them saying, let us try again.

She rolled over in the bed, her long black braids a lump at the back of her head. She'd slept curled around her pillows again, and her limbs unfolded slowly in the early morning dark. She thought about ignoring the birdsong, she thought about crumpling herself up again, pulling up the duvet around her shoulders, closing her eyes and falling back into oblivion. But that was dangerous, she knew. Better to get up, to get on with it, to try again than to give in before she'd even started.

It was good to have the birds depending on her. It meant

she had to get up. It wasn't so much that she cared about them one way or the other, though she supposed somewhere inside herself she did. It was more that they would cry and call and cry and call till she got up, drew the silk from their cages, looked to their seed and their water, and finally gave them a task. They were canny creatures. They knew what they were about. They wanted a job.

Leah opened her eyes fully and looked again at the cages. She could see the outline of one plump bird. Sandy, she thought. She's pressed right up against the bars of her cage again. Leah let her hands slide down her body in their regular morning inventory, gliding over plump breasts, belly, hips and thighs. Still there, she told herself. Still all there. At least on the outside. She peeled back the duvet and swung herself up to sitting, feet planted square on the floor. She felt she had to move with authority, since it seemed to be the only thing that could get her moving and keep her moving at all these days. She sat for a moment, hands resting on bare knees. She wanted nothing more than to freefall back into the pillows, but she knew this torpor wasn't helping. It fed itself, this inactivity.

"Just get up and write the note," she said out loud. "Do that much, then see about the rest. Do that much, and see where you are."

She shivered in the cold room and pulled her bathrobe on over her skin. She didn't like the birds to see her naked. They made her skin crawl. All birds did, with their buggy feathers and beady eyes, and the way they seemed to have ideas about things. These two were no different, and were, in fact, perhaps a bit worse. They were intelligent, that was part of it, intelligent enough, anyhow, to find their way out every day and their way back again every night. And though she needed them for that, valued them for that, it still unnerved her to have such sentient beings living in cages on her bookcase. She thought naming them would help. Sandy and Harold they were. But it only made things worse. Once they were named, they seemed to develop personalities. Sandy was a go-getter; Harold more even-tempered, more laidback, but still, he got the job done. He was a plodder; Sandy liked to shake things up. And once they had names and personalities, things seemed to go downhill for Leah. She was reconsidering the ethics of keeping them in a cage, but the alternative—letting them have the run of the house—was too horrifying to contemplate. She worked hard to hide her revulsion from them, but she lived in fear that her careful facade would slip and that someday soon, Sandy and Harold would divine the truth. Leah hated the birds, but she needed them, desperately.

Sandy began to scold as Leah moved toward the cages. She pulled the red silk covers off and fixed the birds with what she hoped was a cool gaze. She wondered if she was fooling them. The look on Sandy's face indicated otherwise. But Harold was just as placid as ever. She began to think she preferred the male bird, but of course, that was nothing new, and she had to admit such preferences were the root of a number of her troubles. And also, he was a pigeon, and she would do well to keep things in perspective. His brain was the size of a piece of gravel, if that, and whatever personality he seemed to have was certainly her own projection. She shook some seed into the feeding dishes in the cages, disengaged the water bottles and took them to the bathroom sink, where she rinsed and refilled them.

She popped them back in their brackets and said, "It won't be long, now, guys. Let me just make the coffee and think about it some, and I'll get you set up before too long. Just hang in there."

She didn't know when she'd started talking like a folksy camp councillor, but she had, and there it was. Not much she could do about it now, and besides, she really didn't talk to very many people these days, so what did it matter how she sounded? She was pretty sure the birds didn't care, and if they did—oh well. They were birds. They would simply have to cope.

She padded down the stairs to the kitchen and in her head she began to compose that day's note. She wondered about striking the right tone. She wanted to be forceful but not too aggressive. It was important, she felt, to proceed with caution. And though she had not yet received a reply or really a sign of any kind, the birds, at least, returned to her with their note sheaths empty, so she had to assume the letters were hitting their mark. She *decided* to assume they were, rather. It was better that way.

In the kitchen, she scooped coffee beans into the grinder, pushed the lid down and flipped the switch. The sudden noise made the cat jump, and she said, "It's okay buddy, it's just the coffee grinder. Same thing every morning, right?"

Jesus, I'm turning into Saint Francis of Assisi, she thought but didn't say. She was already doing a fair bit of talking out loud when she was alone, and sure, she could pass it off as talking to the birds or the cat, but she was only marginally comfortable with that. She dumped the ground coffee into the basket filter, filled the pot with water, poured that into the machine, flipped the switch and waited for the familiar burbling and the soothing aroma. She didn't even care anymore if she actually drank a cup of coffee, but making it had become very important. It was a thing people did in the morning, and so she would do it and it would help keep her on track. At least, that was the plan. So far it had worked, but she had to admit she didn't hold out a lot of hope for it long-term. Still, she tried not to be pessimistic too far into the future. She tried to keep her crabbing to a situational basis. Not always easy, but a worthy goal to strive for, she thought.

As the coffeemaker cranked and groaned, she leaned against the counter and drew a pencil from the pocket of her robe. She twirled it between her fingers and thought. The cat leapt lightly from his perch on the rocking chair in the corner and stretch-walked across the kitchen toward her, purring intently. He got up close and wound around her ankles a bit, purring the entire time.

"You want crunchies?" she asked him, in a completely superfluous way. It was obvious what he wanted, and inevitable that she would put out. She scooped out a cup of dry food and slid it into his bowl. He immediately abandoned her ankles and applied himself to his breakfast, eating noisily. This left her free to think. She tapped the pencil's eraser end against her teeth, tasting a hint of the rubber. It made her think of September, the real new year, the true time of renewal. How she longed for the feeling she got from a fresh package of lined loose-leaf paper. Or the ever-expanding realm of the possible represented by a new box of pencil crayons, their points all uniform and perfcct. But what she felt instead was the grubbiness of mid-winter, all brown snow and chapped lips, and scarf that smelled like four months worth of expelled breath trapped forever in synthetic fibres. She sighed and closed her eyes. Maybe she should go back to bed after all. Turn off the coffeemaker, put the silk back over the cages, slip back into bed and back into dark unconsciousness. But no, she'd done that already, for too many days. She had to work on the project. She had to at least write the note.

She pulled a square of royal blue paper from the pack of origami sheets on the counter. She licked the end of the pencil as she'd seen it done in old movies. She didn't notice if it had any effect on the graphite, but she'd grown to like the ritual, and, a little bit, she'd grown to like the taste. She thought for a moment, elbows leaning on the countertop, her butt sticking out and swaying gently, absently. Finally, her hand began to move over the square of paper. *After midnight*, she wrote, *in the silence, intensive, the machines turned away discreetly, as if to grant you privacy at last.* She stopped writing, looked over at the cat, who sat back from his bowl and licked his paw. She looked back at what she'd written, hesitated for a moment and then nodded. "Okay," she said out loud. "Alright. Okay."

She folded it into a little frog and, cradling it in the palm of her hand, climbed the stairs once more to her bedroom where the birds waited, one trusting, and one impatient, for her to return.

. . .

In the house next door, Henry sat in his boxer shorts; his guitar perched on his knee, one hand around its neck. A joint burned in the saucer on the floor, and Henry scratched his belly absently with his free hand. There was a lot going on, that was for sure, but he knew he had to try to stay on schedule. He looked again at the song list taped to the side of his guitar, to its shapely hip. He shook his hair out behind him, thinking it might help to clear his head. He strummed a few experimental chords, cleared his throat, gazed out the window. Waited to feel that the moment was upon him, waited to feel like it was time to get to it. And get to it he must. If he didn't practise, he couldn't play, and if he didn't play, he'd never get a record deal. And without a record deal he'd be just another dirty hippie working at the juice bar forever. Or selling hemp bracelets on the street, playing hacky sack between customers. Oh god, how he did not want that for his life. He was projecting big things for himself, big things. But projecting wasn't enough. He had to actually produce. He looked at the joint still smoking in the saucer. Part of the problem, he wondered, or part of the solution? He wasn't going to figure it out today, that was for sure. He was already too high for that. He plucked it out of the saucer, took one more drag and pinched it out. Time to stop fucking around, he thought. What's first on the list? He strummed again, A, then G. And then he was away, at last and thank fuck, he thought. Here we go. He put his whole body into it, closed his eyes a little and leaned toward his instrument as if it were a beautiful girl he couldn't get enough of.

. . .

Leah stopped mid-climb on the stairs. There it was again, that song. She froze, thinking of Nathan, thinking of what Psychic Sue had said. "When you hear that song," she said Nathan was saying, "it's me singing it for you." Leah leaned her head against the cool, smooth plaster of the wall that joined her house to the house next door and wished that were so. If only she were climbing the stairs to find her brother sitting on the chair in the study, lovely blond guitar on his lap, his hands moving over the strings, his voice not quite doing justice to the tune. If only the strains of that song were coming from her kitchen, her backyard, from the living or dining room. If only Nathan were here in the shower singing, knocking her down the way he did when they were kids, putting his knees on her arms and pinning her to the floor, typing the words out on her chest. If only it were he singing the words that always made her cry, then teasing her about being a crybaby. If only that. She clutched the royal blue paper frog between her fingers. *If you could read my mind, love, what a tale my thoughts could tell. Just like an old time movie, bout a ghost from a wishing well*. The voice through the wall was warm and aching and Leah let it wash over her. She wanted to be free of it, of all of it. The paper frog in her hand felt heavy. If only she had some assurance that the project was the right one, that it stood any chance of working. She took a deep breath and tapped her head once, a little harder than gently, against the wall.

Sandy was whirting and cooing louder than ever. Leah sighed and started her climb anew.

. . .

Nathan paced. It felt like all he knew how to do anymore. And it made him feel better to take the library lawn in lengths, his fists balled to keep him from flapping his arms the way he had as a child. It helped him to think. He paced endlessly, arms straight, fists balled, bottom lip pulled in. It was a nice place to pace, actually. A wide sidewalk cut into the lawn diagonally, from Spring Garden Road on one side, to Grafton on the other. If he was feeling like a change, he could pace the shorter path from the library steps to Brunswick Street. He tried to do this only during the day, though. The route took him a bit behind the old stone building, away from people. It made him nervous to be away like that, to be out of sight, and to have passersby and strangers hidden to him. He preferred the busyness of the longer path and stuck mainly to it. Also, it was close to the statue of Winston Churchill and when he could stand to have his arms folded behind him instead of straight at his sides, Nathan liked occasionally to walk like the great man, though he didn't find it changed the quality of his thoughts at all. When he got tired, he sat on the steps, and they were fine steps for sitting. Now and again he would slip into the library when someone else pulled open its heavy wooden doors. Inside, he'd browse the aisles of fiction, looking for murder mysteries he hadn't read and running his long thin fingers over the spines of first editions and Faulkner books he'd loved. He didn't read much these days though. Titles, mostly, and now and again the book reviews pinned to the bulletin board. He just didn't have the patience for reading, he found. Besides he didn't have a library card and the service at the main branch was terrible. The sulky teens with their cystic acne, their multiple piercings, their unhappiness. He couldn't get them to focus on him long enough to tell him he'd need two pieces of ID to get a library card, and anyway, he didn't know what had happened to his ID, so it wasn't worth it. He would only come into the library for a change of scenery or for company if there wasn't much happening out on the paths or the steps. Besides, he didn't want to miss a delivery, and as far as he knew, the bird wouldn't try to come inside. Someone would have to open the door for it anyhow, and then once it was in, how would he get it out? It was too much to think about. He'd just spend most of his time outside, waiting for them. It was okay. It didn't bother him. And the bird mostly arrived around the same time every day, so he could just make sure he was out there at the right time and it'd be no problem.

It was a little warmer today, so the chip trucks were out, lining Spring Garden Road, along with the hippies and the homeless kids—harder and harder to tell them apart these days, they were equally grubby and foul-tempered, even the hippies were kind of mean, which didn't seem right somehow, but what the hell did Nathan know? He'd always been ridiculously straight, though those who loved him found it an endearing quality.

"It's against the law," Rebecca used to say to him. "That's your mantra: It's against the law. So straight, my sweet straight boy." It was true Nathan had a healthy respect for the law. He had even studied it for a little while, though he suspected, even when he was going to class, that he loved police procedurals and lawyer movies more than he actually loved the law. It seemed like a slender thing to base a career on, especially given how hard law school was proving to be and how many lives might depend on his success were he to practise as a defence lawyer. Or even as a prosecutor. The whole thing was frankly ridiculous. He loved to argue and debate, that was one thing. And he was freakishly logical, that was another. Plus, he was done his math degree, and Rebecca still had several years of school left, and he wanted to be where she was, and she was at school. So, sure, law, why not?

After a while he realised he was never going to be a lawyer and he just went to the classes because he was interested. It made things a lot more fun for him, and for Rebecca too. He mellowed right out and let her be the stressed out one. He stopped caring about his homework and just listened compassionately when she bitched about hers. He read a lot and played his guitar and thought about asking her to marry him, even though they fought like children. There was something about the way she ran her hand over his collarbone, the way she seemed to memorise the sweep of his skeleton that made the little door in his heart swing open whenever she was around. Oh, god, Rebecca. He didn't know when he would see her again. It was like a hole in his heart to be away from her like this. To be away from everybody. He staggered to a stop in his pacing, his arms wrapped around his chest. He closed his eyes tight and pulled both lips inside his mouth, head bowed to the ground. It hurt, it hurt. People jostled him as they went by, but he barely felt it. He stood there in front of the Spring Garden Road library near the statue of Winston Churchill and he wept.

. . .

"I'm coming, I'm coming," she snarked as she got to the top of the stairs. "Don't get your feathers in a... flap. Heh. Oh god. Now I'm making puns to the pigeons. This is getting out of hand." She strode into the bedroom and took Sandy's cage down from the bookcase.

"Fine, fine," she said. "I will set you free." She attached the small paper frog to Sandy's left leg and carried her over to the window. "Happy now?" she asked. The bird gave her a baleful glance. "Jesus," she muttered. "This cannot go on."

She gave Sandy's plump body a little squeeze, swallowing the revulsion that arose in her throat. She pulled up the sash and leaned her head out the window. The air smelled like snow, which made Leah's heart sink. Surely it was almost spring. Surely to Christ this winter would end sometime. Sandy made a little *birt* sound and wriggled in Leah's hand.

"Yes, yes," Leah said, "I hear you." She extended her arm out the window and thrust her hand quickly upward, freeing the pigeon as she did.

"Godspeed," she muttered as the bird took flight, its greyish-brown wings stretching out over the neighbourhood, the tiny blue frog attached to her leg marking her. Leah watched her go, feeling a little admiration for the bird's fine form in spite of herself. "Godspeed," she said again, then drew in her head and pulled the window closed. In his cage, Harold sat looking sad but resigned.

"It's just for a few hours," Leah said guiltily. "You know she'll be right back." Harold clucked forlornly and turned to face the wall. "Oh for chrissakes," she said. "You're just a bird." But she knew it was much more than that, and that bird or not, there was a bond between Harold and Sandy. Indeed, this was what made them so valuable to Leah, what made it possible for her to do what she needed to, in the way she needed to. It was what made it okay that she hadn't been outside in almost two weeks. Well, maybe not okay exactly, certainly not if you asked Charlotte, which Leah purposefully did not. But Charlotte being Charlotte, she was only too happy to step up and tell Leah straight out that she did not think it was okay that Leah was holed up, living in her bathrobe and eating nothing but goat cheese and crackers. She did not think it was okay for an instant. Yes, she had helped Leah obtain the birds, but she'd only done it because Leah had been so insistent, and if she'd known what the result was going to be, if she'd known Leah was going to stop washing her hair, and refuse to even go downtown for one little drink after Charlotte's most trying day at work ever, she never would have agreed to help. And she hoped—no, expected—that Leah would put a stop to her foolishness soon. And it was foolishness, Charlotte didn't mind saying. Charlotte never minded saying, which was one of the things Leah found so appealing about her. But these days, more and more, Leah found she wished Charlotte felt some compunction to keep her thoughts to herself, even just a little. Leah was finding it hard enough just to get up in the morning and write the notes, she certainly didn't need to be harangued about her hair or whatever was setting Charlotte off on any given day. She did, however, need Charlotte to bring her fresh supplies of goat cheese and crackers, and things for her recipes, and Charlotte did have a nice way of including a bottle of vodka or scotch on the grocery list, and though she was also a little creeped out by the birds, Charlotte was good about hanging out for a bit, mixing a drink or two and sticking around for a chat. Leah knew she wasn't much company these days; it was just that she was focused on her project. And she knew she was lucky to have a friend like Charlotte who just took Leah's latest weirdness in stride. Yes, she rolled her eyes a lot, but at least she rolled them to Leah's face. And that meant something.

Leah didn't know why, exactly, she'd stopped being able to go outside. She'd felt a kind of wide-open vertigo once she realised Nathan had gotten loose. And all she could think afterward was, gotta get home, gotta get home. She hurried along North Park Street in front of the Armoury, its old stone walls perpetually held up by scaffolding. She hurried in front of the new condos on the corner, their new stone walls perpetually defaced by graffiti. Along Moran Street her back prickled as she pulled her keys from her pocket. She fumbled urgently with the lock, threw open the door and dashed inside, slamming the door behind her.

The panic still tingled in her veins, and she whipped through the house, turning on lights, even though it was barely four o'clock, and muttering aloud. She cast a glance into each corner of the house, as if to give a warning to whatever might dwell there. I'm not unaware, those glances seemed to say, this is me putting you on alert. She didn't think about it, she just did it. She had to. And later, when the panic had subsided, she pretended there hadn't been any panic at all. That Nathan wasn't loose—it was too ridiculous to even think about—Nathan was dead. Her imagination was overactive. She'd seen him because she'd wanted to see him, and now she wasn't seeing him because; well, because he was dead. That was all.

But that wasn't all, as it turned out. While it was true that Nathan was dead, and that her imagination was overactive, she knew something had changed. She could feel it in the air around her front door. It was sinister and forbidding. She could open the door to get the mail, and she could even venture out onto the porch to bring in the newspaper if she had to. But she felt that same prickling panic if she thought about going any further, leaving her front step. And so she'd snatch up the mail, snatch up the newspaper, dart back inside and slam the door.

But Nathan stayed loose. He didn't come back to her, and the feeling that he was out there somewhere didn't dissipate. And eventually, Leah came to realize that she was going to have to find a way to bring him back, without leaving her house at all.

So when Charlotte told her about the birds, she knew what she had to do. Or, rather, what she had to ask Charlotte to do for her.

The night Charlotte went to get the birds was cold and clear. Darkness was beginning to whisper over the city, though the harbour was still bright as she came across Citadel Hill. She jammed her hands into her pockets and hoped she wasn't on a fool's errand. One-Eyed Carl, for chrissakes. Homing pigeons, of all things. Still, she had only herself to blame. She'd seen the ad for the birds in the *Pennysaver* during a marathon laundry session. She'd mentioned them to Leah. She'd been kidding about the birds being a solution to Leah's problem. She should have known Leah would take it seriously, though. She hadn't, sadly, thought far enough down that particular road to realise that Leah's reluctance to leave the house meant that she herself would have to carry out this errand, but hey, that's what friends are for, right? She smiled grimly, and hoped Carl wouldn't be any weirder than was altogether necessary.

Dim lights shone on the library path. Winston Churchill cast a half-hearted shadow on the lawn before him as Charlotte rounded the corner, her boots crunching on the thin layer of snow that covered the path. A kid in a dirty bandanna and a huge parka stood near the steps, shifting from one foot to the other in the cold and shrugging his shoulders repeatedly, making the parka jump and slide. "Spare some change?" he said, as Charlotte crunched by.

"Sorry kid," Charlotte said. "I'm on a mission, with exact change." Charlotte looked around the library lawn. "I'm supposed to meet up with a guy named One-Eyed Carl. You wouldn't happen to know him, would you?"

The kid wiped his nose with the back of his hand and nodded. "Yeah, but he's not around right now. He's gone to Montréal, to check out the French girls. He said he might have some luck there."

"Huh," said Charlotte. "I was supposed to meet him here. He was going to sell me something."

The kid looked around furtively, nervously, side to side over his shoulders. "Geez lady," he muttered.

Charlotte laughed. "Oh god, no," she said. "Pigeons, he had a couple of homing pigeons."

"Oh, those," the kid said. "I can help you with those." He bent down and rustled in the bushes behind him, finally drawing out two cages, a little ball of feathers huddled in each. "Twenty bucks," he said, "for the two of them, and there's even a bit of birdseed in the cages to get you started."

"Indeed," Charlotte said. She pulled a twenty from her back pocket. "Tell me," she said, "One-Eyed Carl...is that for real? For real he has one eye?"

"Nah," the kid said. "He just makes us call him that. He thinks it makes him sound tough. You want these birds, or what?"

"Yeah," Charlotte said, "I want the birds." She handed him the twenty and picked up the cages. "Thanks man." She started to turn away, cages in hand, then thought better. "Listen," she said, putting down the cages and reaching into her pocket. "You smoke?"

"Yeah," the kid said, "so what?"

"So, here's a cigarette, that's what. And furthermore, you around here much?"

"Every day," the kid said, his parka bunched up almost to his ears.

"Right." Charlotte pulled out a lighter, lit the kid's cigarette. "Keep an eye peeled for these birds, okay? They'll be back around here, probably once a day. The guy they're here for, he's...kind of slow. If you see one of these birds hanging around, you might need to pitch in, okay?"

"Meaning?" the kid asked. The cigarette hung from his lip.

"Meaning," Charlotte said, picking up the cages again, "if you see one of these birds back here, with a message on its leg, you might need to take it off and I don't know, put it —" she looked around the library lawn. "Put it in those bushes." She gestured to a low stand of evergreens that hugged the front wall of the old stone building. "Okay?"

The kid shrugged. "What's in it for me?"

Charlotte sighed. The things she did. "I'll stop by every couple of days, see how you're doing, and throw you a couple bucks, okay?"

"And cigarettes?'

Charlotte rolled her eyes. "And cigarettes, yes, alright. Jesus Christ."

"Deal," the kid said. He put his hand out.

Charlotte gestured, a cage in each hand. "Deal," she said.

. . .

Henry put his guitar aside, leaning it against the doorframe. When he wasn't holding it, his fingers itched for contact, but sometimes, it was too much. Sometimes it was so intense it burned. And these days, the songs were giving him so much trouble he just had to put the instrument aside now and again and move around a bit. Especially when he'd been playing all day long, the same songs again and again. Times like these he'd roam the length of the house's upper floor and if that didn't calm him down, he'd take the stairs two at a time, up and down, up and down. That usually soothed him enough that he could get back to writing or rehearsing or whatever was proving difficult that day. When the going got particularly tough, he'd resort to smoking. But these days, he was trying to walk it off first.

He was on his third lap of the top floor—bathroom, hall-way, landing, study, landing, hallway, bathroom—when the phone rang.

"Thank Christ," he said, scrambling for the cordless. "Thank Christ," he said again as he answered it.

There was a moment of silence, then the voice of Johnny Parker. "Man, I don't know who you were expecting, but it's just me, dude."

Johnny was by no means Henry's oldest friend, but in many ways, he was his most important. It wasn't that Johnny had influence, because he didn't. He was pretty much where Henry was in that regard. But Johnny had something else, and Henry was hard-pressed to name it, exactly. It had something to do with the amount of time they'd known each other. A little under ten years, but they'd been ten formative years. The three years in school and the six or seven since, a couple of long-term relationships each, followed inevitably by as many nasty break-ups, followed, of course, by a lot of drinking and cussing and staying out late, all night if necessary. And a lot of shit-talking and bluster and locker room crap too. They'd get together when they were both in town and exchange road stories, and though on the outside it sounded like the sad bravado of a couple of rootless road-pigs, Henry knew it was really their way of staying connected to each other and to their own sanity. He would never express this, in so many words to Johnny Parker. Hell, he'd barely even describe it to himself in that way. But he knew, at the bottom of his road-pig heart, that it was true. Johnny Parker understood him in a way no one else had or could. Truth was Johnny Parker understood him in a way that Henry longed to be understood. It was understood between them that this was a strictly off-limit topic of conversation, but sometimes, sometimes, Henry longed to say it aloud.

Now, though, he simply said, "How're you?"

"Crazy, man," Johnny Parker said. "I'm fucking crazy. How're you?"

"Was about to go over the side before you called man. Wanna get a drink?"

"Thought you'd never ask," Johnny Parker said. "See you there?"

"Damn straight," Henry said, and clicked off the phone.

He rummaged through the pile of clothes on the bathroom floor and wondered when he'd stop living that way. Damp shirts and pants embraced each other; socks and underwear clung to each other in mildewed clumps. It was horrifying, he knew, and it didn't use to be this way. And even though he knew it would pass, knew he'd get back to his usual slightly-messy-but-not-health-code-violating ways, knew this was just a way of getting back at Tina and sure, at himself, for her leaving, knew, ultimately, that this was just play-acting, that didn't make it better right now. It didn't make him feel any better about sifting through the fetid pile for the least offensive shirt, the darkest pants so they wouldn't show the dirt, a pair of socks that didn't make him weep with despair. The underwear he'd given up on. He'd go commando, no big deal. There was no way he was putting those grey jockey shorts next to his skin. He imagined himself chucking all the stuff in the big old claw-foot tub, running a warm bath, dissolving detergent in it and just letting the stuff soak all day, but it was too much effort now. Maybe when he got home. Maybe when his edges were a little blunted by alcohol and conversation and proximity to

Johnny Parker and a bar full of pretty girls who thought the two of them could show pretty girls a good time. But now? Too much like reality for him.

He managed to scrape together a shirt that, though damp, smelled only slightly, and a pair of black jeans that seemed to be alright. Socks, socks, socks were a problem. It was too cold to go without, so he grabbed a pair of thick grey work socks and turned the hairdryer on them. They sailed out in his hand like nubbly flags, and the warm blowing air felt nice against his skin. Once the socks were toasty, he pulled them on his feet and shoved his feet immediately into his boots. If he just didn't think about what was going on in there, he figured he'd be okay. He grabbed his leather jacket off the newel post at the bottom of the stairs and slammed out the door to meet Johnny.

· · ·

The teacups rattled on their shelves as Leah waited for Sandy to come home. She flinched at the sound, imagining the delicate bone china she'd inherited from her grandmother shifting and chipping in the cabinet. She wasn't sure which neighbour it was who kept doing that, but if she ever left the house again, she planned to give him a piece of her mind.

She was on the couch in the living room wrapped in blankets and afghans. The window was open upstairs against Sandy's return, and the house was chilly. Leah was loath to crank the furnace up though. She could hear her father's voice in her head: Close the door   goddamnit; we can't heat the whole neighbourhood. She wished she had a fireplace or a woodstove or less guilt about just firing up the heat, but there it was. Two pairs of socks, a sweater so thick she could hardly move her arms to turn pages, and a pile of blankets weighing on her legs like a fallen tree pinning her to the couch.

She'd been reading through her stack of home decorating magazines, but none of them had what she was looking for. Not that she expected to find plans for an urban aviary, necessarily, but you never knew, these days, and besides, she figured she could adapt some other project from the glossy pages. If only she had an attic, she thought, she could leave the window open up there, insulate the ceiling like crazy and make sure the opening was tight as a drum.

Sadly, there was no attic in the house, and she was getting tired of freezing her ass off. It was fine during the day, especially the days, like this one, when she managed to work. She'd spent the morning and most of the afternoon testing a particularly tricky cheese soufflé recipe, and refining an oatmeal and apricot cookie recipe. The house filled with comforting odours, and the heat from the oven and Leah's own raised temperature, from actually moving around, chopping and stirring, made it easy to forget that upstairs, a window was open to the wintry afternoon. In fact, if the recipe was particularly challenging, Leah could forget, for a moment, for the time it took to mince an onion, say, or clarify a stick of butter, that things were not as simple as adding flour to melted butter and stirring to make a roux, and then adding stock and watching it thicken. In real life, in her real life, equations were not that simple. Not that straightforward. Definitely not that dependable.

Once the day's cooking was done, once the soufflé was sitting on the counter, waiting for Charlotte to come over and eat it, once the cookies were packaged up and put in the freezer in the hopes that some day soon Leah would feel like eating them, once the sun started to sink in the western sky, that's when Leah felt it the most. Felt the cold streaming in through that open window. Felt the exhaustion that came not with a day well spent on hard work, but rather with the endless fretting and planning and scheming she did around the notes, and the birds and the whole damn project.

What she was really doing, she knew, what was really wearing her out as she lay there on the couch, was simply waiting for Nathan to come back or go on. Waiting for it to happen, waiting to know it had. Straining to feel him around her, or feel him leave. She knew, by now, that he was at the library. Knew it the way she'd known he was missing in the first place. She wished she could be sure he was getting the messages—that he was receiving them and understood what they meant. She wished he'd send just one note back, just one word, even, scrawled on a piece of cigarette package, a grease spotted paper bag that had once held french fries, anything that would let her know she was hitting the mark, that he understood she was sorry, that he understood what he was and what he had to do. But there had been no message from him, and so far, there was no way for her to know if she was getting through to him. She closed her eyes and concentrated, but still, she felt nothing. Eventually her breathing turned deep and even and she was asleep again.

. . .

As he crunched across the darkening Common, Henry felt his pockets for a cigarette. Fuck. He'd left them at home. Whatever. He'd just buy another pack downtown. He felt for his wallet. Double fuck. That was at home, too. He stopped short, sighed deeply. He jammed his hands down into his cold leather pockets, turned around and trudged back to the house.

. . .

Nathan sat on the library steps; the bird perched beside him. He patted her head and dreaded the moment she'd take wing again and leave him. He thought about the collection of little paper animals piling up in the bushes against the library. He didn't pretend to understand what was going on. All he knew was that each day, the bird arrived. And each day, the kid in the parka took a brightly coloured paper animal off its leg and hid it in the bushes. And then he took off, but the bird hung around, flying over to Nathan where he paced near Winston Churchill, or hopping around beside him where he rested on the steps. They spent an hour or more a day together, just sitting, enjoying each other's company.

And then, once the bird took off too, Nathan would tuck himself in between the bushes and the library and look at that day's arrival. So far, there was an orange fish, a red monkey, a green cat and a gold bird. Today's delivery had been a blue frog. There was something so familiar about the forms. He imagined they must mean something, taken all together, but he couldn't think what, much less could he figure out who might be sending them or for whom they were intended. The kid in the parka didn't seem very interested in them. The most he did was hide them away.

But there was something about their shapes that soothed Nathan, their simple paper lines, the love they seemed to emanate. And anyway, the bird always came directly to him afterward, which made him think perhaps the animals were supposed to be his. And lately, the bird had been staying with him more and more. He even thought she seemed a little reluctant to leave, especially tonight. He stroked the sleek, smooth feathers knitted across her back and sang gently to her, the way he used to sing to himself, or for Leah or Rebecca. He wished he had his guitar, but that, like his ID, had gone missing. It was on the tip of his mind, the whereabouts of his things. He knew he'd see them again, though, once he got everything figured out. Till then, he'd have to make do with just his voice, and the likes of the pigeon for company. It was getting dark though, and the bird seemed ready to get down to business. She straightened up out of her comfortable slump and waggled her tail feathers.

"Okay," he said to her, "I understand. And I'll see you again, right? Tomorrow? Or maybe the next day?" The bird plucked at her own feathers with her little pink beak and shook herself again. "Okay then," Nathan said. "See you. Safe flight! And thanks for the frog."

The bird hopped a few steps toward Brunswick Street before leaping into the air and spreading her wings. Nathan watched her go up over the rooftops of the café, the furniture store, the candy store and the wine boutique. He watched her wing towards Citadel Hill until he could no longer make her out against the darkening clouds.

"Safe flight," he said again, even though there was no way she could hear him at that distance. "Thanks again."

He stood a moment staring after her. Then he let out a deep breath, curled his hands into fists and began his nightly route. He paced the path from Spring Garden down to Grafton, turned and paced back, stopping now and again to contemplate Winston Churchill, but never for very long.

. . .

Henry let himself in, turning his key in the sticky lock. Now he had to pee, as well, and he hated being slowed down like that. "Come on, come on," he said as he jiggled the key. Finally the lock gave, and he was inside. He undid his zipper with one hand while he jogged to the bathroom. He leaned against the wall as the warm urine streamed out ahead of him.

"Wallet, wallet, wallet," he repeated aloud. "Where the fuck did I leave that thing?" He tried to picture it in a pant pocket or on the bureau in James and Emily's room, but he couldn't conjure up its image. He hadn't felt it among his mouldering clothes on the floor of the upstairs bathroom, and he was pretty sure he didn't have the heart to go through that again. If it came to that, he'd simply have to sponge off Johnny Parker, no two ways. "Think, think," he said, as the stream of urine slowed to a trickle. He shook his dick off, stuffed it back in his jeans and zipped up carefully. The last thing he needed was a commando-meets-zipper incident. That'd really put a damper on his night. Damper, he thought. The wallet is on the floor in the living room in front of the woodstove. He'd passed out there last night, and remembered taking the wallet out of his pocket before he drifted off. It had been an uncomfortable lump between his ass and the floor. His smokes were probably there, too, come to think of it.

Sure enough, they were. He grabbed them up, stuffed them in his pocket, remembered his keys, and slammed out the door again.

The bird caught him by surprise, swooped down almost taking his head off. "Fuck is that?" he shouted as it turned and flew up to the second floor window next door. "Jesus bird," he sputtered nonsensically. "Christ could have killed me." He scowled up at it as it squeezed in the half-open window. "Fucking pigeon," he said. "Fucking going in through the window! The hell? Fuck." His heart was pounding like a snare drum in his chest. "Jesus, someone should do something about that," he shouted toward the offending house. Then he jumped down the three steps to the sidewalk and jogged back toward the Common. Johnny Parker would be waiting, and at this rate, he'd be half in the bag and half in bed with some young cutie by the time Henry even got downtown. Jesus wept.

. . .

Leah bolted awake. What was all the yelling? The neighbourhood was seriously going down hill all of a sudden. Ever since James and Emily had gone to England, whoever they had living in their house was sure doing a lot of loud swearing and slamming. It was driving Leah nuts. It was almost enough to make her leave the house, she thought.

Neil stretched into the room, paused in the doorway and arched his back. Leah smiled at him and he looked back at her, his eyes glowing iridescent. He yawned hugely and let out a squeaky meow at the same time. Heart melting stuff, even if right after he looked like he would take her down and eat her.

"You might as well forget it," Leah said. "Who would pull the fur on your back for you, hmmm?" She reached over and grabbed a nice handful of Neil's ample back-flesh. She pulled it up, like taffy, and he purred appreciatively. "Or pour your crunchies? You need me, Neily Neilerson," she chided. "Don't forget it."

Above the purring of the orange cat, she heard the flapping from upstairs that signalled Sandy's return. She swallowed the wave of fresh and immediate fear and revulsion that washed over her at the thought of a bird in the house, letting it be replaced by a mixture of relief and anticipation. Was tonight the night Nathan would send a message back? Had he, himself, somehow come back with Sandy? Leah stopped, cocked her head, listened. She didn't hear anything but feathers and flapping, but then, Nathan had been silent, in the conventional way. She stood still and tried to feel him, but there was nothing. She breathed out. Still, maybe he'd sent a message. She took the stairs two at a time, got to her bedroom to find Sandy turning round and round in her cage, as if showing Harold that she was alright, everything was okay, nothing to worry about now that she was home. And Harold did look relieved, with his little beady eyes and his snubbed beak, his greyish-brown feathers tousled on his head as if he'd just woken up, as if they'd been displaced by some avian pillow.

Leah got up close, looked for a message on Sandy's leg. Nothing. At least the blue frog was gone. Maybe it had simply fallen off, she thought, panicking. Maybe there was a trail of origami creatures strewn from here to Brunswick Street, lost in the snow, bleeding their vivid colours onto the ground. She snapped the overhead light on for a closer look at the bird. No clues there. She looked deep into Sandy's depthless eyes, for as long as she could stand it. The bird looked—trustworthy. Nervous, but ultimately true. Straight as an arrow. And the holster was secure; Leah had checked it and checked it. She knew she was just being foolish now, just looking for trouble where none existed, looking for explanations where none existed. She would simply have to be patient. She had fucked things up, and if she was going to unfuck things, she'd have to accept that it would take time, that her plan was sound, that Nathan was where he was for a reason, that he'd answer her when he was good and ready, that the bird was reliable. It was a lot of things to take on faith, but really, she didn't see what other choice she had. Unless she was prepared to simply walk away, to not even try, to never know the outcome, but that was untenable. She'd already done that once, or practically anyhow. In fact, if you added it up, she'd betrayed Nathan twice already. She was not interested in doing it a third time. And she knew there was no point in freaking out. The bird had done what she could do for the day. Tomorrow's note would have to be clearer and more pointed. It was the only way she knew.

She stuck her finger through the rungs of the cage and patted the air next to Sandy's tail feathers. It was the best she could do for a show of affection, good thing the birds had each other. She measured out some seed and poured it into Sandy's dish, gave some to Harold, though he'd already eaten his evening meal, snapped off the overhead light and went back downstairs to pour herself a drink.

As she passed the study at the top of the stairs, she did her best not to look inside. It was a room of chaos, a place she put the things for which she had no other place. Nathan's first guitar, for instance.

Nathan's first guitar sounded like shit. It wasn't just because he was still learning how to play it. It's that it genuinely was a piece of utter garbage. Special only because his hands had moved over its strings, his fingers had found their places on the fretboard.

The guitar was unremarkable in every way. Leah couldn't even find a manufacturer's mark on it. The neck was worn, the strings now untuneable, she suspected. It had not been played in years. The almost-year since Nathan had died, and who knew how many before that? He'd long moved on to better instruments. This one, he'd played as a teenage enthusiast. A gangly nerd who'd quickly surpassed even his fellow brainers in his advanced math class, Nathan had turned to music as an outlet for his excess mathematical energy. Leah couldn't understand that part of him—math, just the thought of it, made her scalp itch. But Nathan had picked up this old guitar and learned to play it using what he knew of logic and pattern.

The guitar had always been around, as long as they had and longer. It was battered and worn, a terrible instrument, made of little better than pressboard. Their father had given it to their mother the first Christmas they were married. He had bought it from Consumer's Distributing. It had cost twenty-five dollars, which was a lot of money in those days, especially to a young, newly married couple who were saving to buy a house. It was never clear to Leah and Nathan whether their mother actually played the guitar or was even interested in learning. They'd certainly never seen her with it in her hands. But she loved music, sang along with abandon to the radio, raced their father downstairs on Sunday mornings to be the first to reach the stereo and pick the music that would accompany their breakfast. If she won, it was Buddy Holly or the Beatles. If their father got there first it would be Roy Orbison, or worse, Bob Dylan, or worst of all, Al Jolson.

The guitar had sat in the basement for years, leaning in a corner, its pale wood barely glinting. Then Nathan picked it up one night and slowly, painfully, learned to coax songs out of it. He played "Roxanne" by the Police and sang along, his adolescent voice cracking wide open on the high notes. It was the most lugubrious version of the song Leah had ever heard, but here was someone she knew, her own brother, actually playing the guitar and singing. Leah was impressed enough that the song sounded concert hall ready to her. When Nathan went away to university, he used some of the money from his part-time job tutoring math to buy himself a proper guitar. But he took the first one with him, regardless, and it sat in his dorm room and got played once in a while by some drunken friend whose understanding of logic and pattern was similar to Nathan's, though perhaps not as acute. But then again, with all that beer around, it was hard to tell.

When Nathan died, Rebecca gave that first guitar to Leah. "I can't have it around," Rebecca had said, inclining her head toward the instrument, but not looking right at it. "I just can't have it in my house."

It was *my house* already, not *our house* anymore. Leah took the guitar wordlessly by the neck—it had never had a case that she knew of—and carried it out of Rebecca's house. She put it in the backseat of her car where it sat, like a silent passenger, all the way back to Halifax. Once in a while, she'd glance at it in the rearview mirror. She fought with herself to keep from speaking to it.

At first, she'd kept it on a stand she'd bought specially for it, in the living room. But people asked questions, wanted to hear her play it, and she couldn't. She'd never learned. She, like her mother, loved to belt out songs along with the radio, would sing whatever she could whenever she got the chance. But logic and pattern eluded her, always had, and she could not begin to understand where to put her fingers on the fretboard, how to move her other hand over the strings. And then, too, keeping it in the living room just made her sad. Every time she looked at it, every time she had to explain to someone why she had a guitar she couldn't play, it knocked her breathless all over again. So she moved it to the study upstairs, where it leaned, in its stand, against the bookcase that held Nathan's collection of Hardy Boys hardcovers. Rebecca had sent those on the bus six months after Nathan's death. "Was cleaning out the attic," the note she'd sent along read. "Thought you might like these."

The guitar's once bright veneer had grown dull and somewhat tacky. There were shallow gouges across the front of the body, where Nathan's hands had strummed. The wood beneath was grey and dry, and fine splinters stood up out of the gouges. A layer of dust further dimmed the finish. A finer instrument, Leah knew, would be complex in its composition. This one was pasteboard and glue and ink and plastic, instead of inlays of exotic wood and mother of pearl. When she plucked its strings, it honked discordantly. Still, for all it had been discarded, it had once had life, had been the best and most unexpected present beneath a Christmas tree. It had once been played and loved. Had brought pleasure. For longer than was realistic, it had transcended its roots. It had become a finer instrument. In her imagination, if not in her study, it still was.

Leah shook her head, as if to dislodge the sadness that dwelt there. *Downstairs*, she told herself. *A drink*. She needed something straightforward. In the kitchen, she took the bottle of scotch off the hoosier cabinet, twisted the cap off, brought out a short glass. The ice cube trays were frozen together, she pried the top one off with some difficulty, bent the sides back and forth till a few cubes popped up. She dropped a small handful into the glass and poured herself a sloppy two or three fingers of scotch, watched it tumble over the ice to the bottom of the glass, thought about the burn it left in her throat and down to her belly. Her mouth watered. She looked outside, through the kitchen window. The very thought of all that space unbound made her feel queasy. Even her own backyard, fenced and encircled by trees and lilac bushes though it was, felt too exposed. Especially in winter, no green canopy of leaves and lush branches to act as walls and ceiling. Just the austere, sere, severe black fingers of the maple tree, the gnarled claws of the de-leaved lilac bush, the humps of dirt-streaked snow, the barbecue she always forgot to park in the aluminum shed, the shed itself, brown and ugly, a monolith outside the kitchen window that made a frightful noise whenever the wind blew through the yard. She just couldn't. Even the thought of it was enough to bring back the beginnings of that prickling fear. She could feel the tingle at the back of her head, and all along her arms. Besides, it would be cold out there, the adirondack chairs covered with ice and a thin layer of snow, the ground frosty enough to freeze her feet if she stood in one place too long. Better to stay inside, she thought. She went to the back door and leaned her forehead against the glass, looked out on the darkened yard.

Over the fence, lights were on in the neighbours' kitchens. She could see them doing their dishes, clearing up after supper. She could see their mouths going—laughing, singing, talking, fighting. She could almost hear them, she thought, but then she knew that wasn't true. They were too far away. There was too much separating where she stood and where they were. She reached over and turned off the lamp. Dark kitchen, dark window, dark yard. She breathed against the window glass, fogged it and cleared it, breathing out, breathing in, over and over again. In her hand the ice cubes clinked against the tumbler, melted into the scotch, awaited the heat of her mouth. She closed her eyes a moment, opened them again, watched a man swat a woman with a tea towel, playfully she thought, though it was hard to tell without the sound of their laughter. Maybe their faces were creased in anger. She pushed off against the window with her forehead, took a step away, tossed the scotch to the back of her throat with a practised flick of the wrist. Put the glass in the sink, turned on her heel and left the kitchen. It was early, but she climbed the stairs, climbed into bed, fell into sleep, and was gone.

. . .

Nathan sat on the library steps, his arms wrapped around his knees, his toes pointing out. What the hell happened to all my stuff? He wondered. He further thought, who do I know who would know? And finally, he thought, who do I know?

. . .

Johnny Parker caught the barkeep's eye, lifted his hand, nodded. It set into motion an elaborate and age-old ritual, one Johnny Parker could say with confidence was among his favourites. It was right up there with the look he could share with any number of local musicians, a look that led to a tight cluster of guys and usually a girl or two out in an alcove or nook, some sheltered place. A look that led to much lighting and smoking and passing around of pipes and joints and other accoutrements, that led to tangential, hilarious, stuttering conversations punctuated with hard caught-laughing-in-church laughter and various asides and remarks and supplemental tales, and *what-was-I-going-to-say*s and *hang-on-just-a-minute-let-me-relight-this-fucker*s. He loved it, all of it. And loved too the even older ritual, also set in motion with a look, but this one a more private glance, though it could easily happen across a crowded bar, or even in that selfsame tight cluster smoking up in an alcove or alley. This look, though, was the one that led to wet kisses on the way home and the fast shedding of clothes once there. That was a pretty good ritual, too, he thought. He looked around the bar, there were plenty of girls tonight, some Johnny Parker had already kissed, some he wished he had and some he wouldn't if his career depended on it. Well, maybe then. Fuck, he hoped it never came to that, hoped he'd never have to choose. Anyhow. Where the fuck was Henry? Guy was never on time.

The bartender brought Johnny's drink, tequila and orange juice. Johnny nodded and slid a five across the damp bar, bringing the ritual to an end. Till next time. One sip in, Johnny felt a hand on his shoulder. "Finally," he said, not bothering to look up. "Thought you'd fucked off on me."

"Never," Henry said. "Damn near got killed by a bird, is all, on the way here. Weirdest thing. Came out of nowhere, swooped right down close over my head, then it went up to the window next door and went inside. Fucking wriggled right in the upstairs window. Damn. Weirdest thing, really."

"Neighbour keeps it as a pet maybe," Johnny said, swallowing his drink. "That or the birds are taking over the neighbourhood." He raised his glass in Henry's direction. "Best of luck to you if that's the fucking case. You ever see that movie? Fucking creepy. Good thing you're not permanent there. James'll have his fucking hands full, that's certain."

"Keith's," Henry said, nodding at the bartender. "Anybody here?" he asked Johnny Parker.

"Nah," Parker said, "not really. Pretty much what you'd expect."

The bartender slid Henry's beer to him. "Three seventy-five," she said chewing her gum, mouth slightly agape.

"Yeah," Henry said, groping for change in his pocket. He hauled out a handful of loonies and toonies, put the right amount on the bar and slid it toward the gutter. He pulled a cigarette from Johnny Parker's pack, and fished a lighter from his leather jacket. "The hell," said Johnny Parker. "I thought you knocked off those."

"Meh," said Henry. "I did, but that was before I started working on these jeezly songs. Bastards are smoking me. I need an outlet. So. I can always quit again, right? Nothing but time."

Johnny Parker nodded, and lit a cigarette of his own. They smoked for a time in companionable silence, sipping their drinks, looking at girls, nudging each other now and again, nodding at friends and acquaintances, engaging in that careful language of head tilts and half waves, eyebrow expressions and shoulder shrugs that characterised all serious barroom conversations. The night wore on.

· · ·

Leah shifted in her sleep, legs whistling against sheets. She was dreaming. In the dream were birds, clouds, houses and children holding hands. Like a crayoned memory from 1976. She and Nathan clasped their sweaty palms together and traipsed up the quiet suburban crescent. The big dog from across the street barked, its jaws huge and snapping. Nathan tightened his grip on Leah's hand. "It's okay," he said, "I'm right here with you." She smiled, felt safe, but as they got closer to the house where the dog lived Nathan let his hand drop out of hers. "Nathan," she tried to say, but her throat wouldn't open. He looked back at her as he walked through the grass alley between the houses, toward the chain link gate, behind which the dog slavered and snarled. "It's okay," he said again, as he looked over his shoulder at Leah, small on the sidewalk. But clearly it wasn't, for the big dog reared up on its hind legs, reached its massive jaws over the fence and snapped Nathan up almost whole. As Leah watched her brother disappearing into the black jaws, she screamed his name over and over but it was no use. Her voice would go no louder than a whisper, and Nathan was gone for good.

. . .

"So the next thing I know," Johnny Parker pronounced with all the careful precision of a man used to the havoc wrought by six or seven tequilas with orange juice, "the next thing I know, Leo up and disappears, too. Not too long after that, I start to hear sounds."

"Sounds?" Henry looked up from the shape he was tracing in the wet left behind by his fifth beer. Neck, shoulders, hips, ass.

"Sounds," Johnny Parker confirmed, slurping archly on his drink.

"What kind of sounds?" Henry asked, though he figured he knew.

"The kind of sounds that made me get up off my ass and go check it out for myself."

"And?" Henry prodded. Johnny Parker wanted prodding. In Henry's experience prodding Johnny Parker made for, overall, much the better story. He seemed to need it to wind him up. And Henry, poor drunk Henry, was only too glad to oblige.

"So I go downstairs," Johnny Parker says, "I go downstairs, and there's Sleepy Pete giving it to her at one end, and goddamn Leo getting it from her at the other." He said it with a kind of admiration, though whether it was for Leo and Sleepy Pete, for the nameless woman, or for the whole fantastical situation itself wasn't entirely clear.

"Whoa," Henry said. "No shit."

"I shit you not, Henry, my man," Johnny Parker said. "Absofuckinglutely unbefuckinglievable. I mean really unbelievable. Believe what I tell you, my son, it was completely unbelievable."

"I believe you," Henry said, though he wasn't sure he did. Then again, it was entirely possible. In the weeks since Tina had left, it had occurred to Henry that everybody in Halifax and well, well beyond, was having sex but him. And not just sex. Absofuckinglutely unbefuckinglievable sex. Threesomes in downstairs dressing rooms at lousy two-bit bars. Illicit teenage sex in the bushes on the Common after school. Rollicking laughing sex, the kind that came easily, again and again, through the walls of James and Emily's house and kept Henry awake at night. Hell, for all he knew, from the house on the other side, he was hearing goddamn pigeons having sex. Yep, even the birds were doing it. Right there in front of him, and throwing it in his face.

He drained his beer bottle, replaced it noisily on the bar, and belched morosely.

"Jesus fuck, man," Johnny Parker said, as if noticing Henry for the first time. "We've got to get you back out there. You need a woman, now, no fooling around." He swept one arm grandly out from the bar. "What do you like, my son?" he asked, in a voice loudened by booze. "You can have anyone you want."

Henry swallowed the name on the tip of his tongue. It didn't belong there, not anymore, so he chewed it and swallowed it up. He looked around the bar at the female flesh in varying states of display. Midriffs taut and not, all bared before him. Hips in low-cut jeans, their bones jutting out like sirens lounging on the rocks near shore, luring him to his death, his sweet, well-deserved death. He licked his lips, his mouth dry. Breasts bulged from tank tops in all their jiggly mystery, such silly mounds of flesh, but oh, they called his name, he heard them. Hair cascaded down shapely backs, framed between shoulder blades. Or stuck up in adorably tousled tufts, as if fresh from being fucked. He ached. He ached to his bones, to his boner, he ached. He looked at Johnny Parker, smiled miserably.

"There's no one good here," he said. "Let's move. Gotta take a piss first, though." He got up from the bar and sped to the bathroom, eyes on the floor, hands jammed down in his pockets.

· · ·

Harold poked his beak through the bars of his cage and combed through Sandy's feathers, as if looking for something lost. Sandy rolled her eyes at first, but finally, she settled down and made small comfortable sounds as Harold performed his inventory. Headlights moved across the wall, illuminating the cages in a blaze of red. Sandy sighed and tucked her head under her wing while Harold fussed nearby.

. . .

Charlotte adjusted her cowboy hat over her left eye and winked at herself in the mirror. She heard her name being yelled through the bar. She rolled her eyes and slicked on some lip gloss. When she was good and ready she left the bathroom and moved toward the centre of the big, barn-like room. She climbed up on to the mechanical bull, and nodded at Javier to throw the switch. "YeeeeeeHAW," she yelled, one hand on her hat.

. . .

"Because I've told you, like, a thousand times, you dillhole, that's why," the girl said. She was standing in the pool of light on the path, her arms folded in a manner that didn't bode well for anyone who crossed her.

"Yeah well, I forgot," the kid in the parka said, wiping his nose absently across the back of his hand.

"You forgot?" she said, her voice rising. Her hair was streaked with pink, her eyes shaded with bright blue. She seemed to shimmer and sparkle in the bright light. "You forgot?" she screeched. "That's how much I mean to you, you just forgot?"

The kid shifted from one foot to the other, looked down, looked up, looked bored. "Yo, like what do you want from me, yo?"

The girl stared at him, her blue-lined eyes going wide, then narrowing to slits. "From you?" she said. "Nothing. Nothing at all."

She walked away.

"Damn, man," the kid said to her retreating back. "Damn."

. . .

Nathan stood behind Winston Churchill until the girl stormed away. He thought he'd like to give the kid some advice, but the truth was, he didn't have a clue. He and Rebecca fought so much he kind of forgot what it was like not to fight. Half the time, he didn't even know what they were fighting about. Like now, for instance. He couldn't remember what their last fight had been about, but it must have been a doozy, because he hadn't even seen her in what felt like months. He was sure it wasn't though. He was sure she'd come by soon, ready to forgive him. And he was ready to be forgiven. He was sorry. He didn't care what he had to promise, he'd promise it, if she'd promise never to leave him alone for so long again. He leaned his head against Winston Churchill's hip, so cool, and longed for her. Rebecca. On Spring Garden Road, the kid in the parka shuffled away.

. . .

Henry burst out of the doors of The Pool House and stood on the steps, gulping deep breaths of cold air. Johnny clattered out after him, clapped him on the back and said, "Where to, old man?"

Henry coughed out a cloud of beer breath, "Dunno.

Booze Barn?"

"That's my boy," Johnny Parker said. "Booze Barn it is."

Henry loped down the stairs onto Spring Garden Road. He turned his face up to the night and let his mouth hang open. The chill touched his teeth, and the pain of contact throbbed through his mouth.

Johnny slung one arm around Henry's shoulders. "Booze Barn it is," he repeated. "Boys gonna get some ACTION," he shouted to a passing bus, which roared back a cloud of exhaust. "Boys gonna get back in the SWING," he yelled. Across the street giggled a gaggle of girls whose tank tops defied the brisk March temperature. "Back in the SWING," he repeated to this new audience. "Anyone wanna get back in the swing with my boy?"

Henry rolled his eyes and plucked at Johnny's sleeve, but it didn't matter. The girls moved on, still giggling, rubbing their bare arms with their bare hands, their laughter carried back on the midnight air.

Johnny laughed too, and jumped up and down a time or two, clapping Henry on the back and shouting "whoo!" Henry could only smile. There was no changing Johnny Parker, that was certain. And, Henry had to admit, that was part of his charm. In fact, it was a large part of it. No matter how miserable Henry might feel, when he was with Johnny Parker, he always ended up laughing, in spite of himself or otherwise.

They shambled down Spring Garden Road in this manner, punching each other and trading insults.

At the library, they turned to cut across the lawn. By now, Johnny Parker was singing "Brown Sugar" at maximum volume. In the floodlights of the library, his face was red with effort, cold and drink. Henry shivered in the dampness. Goddamn it, he thought, will it be cold forever? It's enough now. Uncle. Let me up. But it didn't seem the cold was fixing to let up. In fact, he thought, it had dropped about ten degrees in the last minute, and now there was a distinct wind blowing up from the harbour. "Fucking winter," he said to Johnny Parker.

"Yeah," Johnny said. "Come on."

They trudged to the library's side door, a secluded little spot out of the wind and mostly out of sight of passersby. Turning their backs to the library lawn, Henry acted as a shield while Johnny sparked up a joint. They passed it back and forth between them, sucking meditatively and mostly keeping quiet, except to bitch about the cold. As they turned to go, a flash of colour caught Henry's eye. A line of small brightly hued animals gathered under the bushes near the side door.

"The fuck," he said. "Check these out."

He crouched down to get a better look. Cat, frog, fish, bird, all made of paper and neatly arranged beneath the lowest boughs of the evergreen shrubbery, sheltered there from the wind.

"Awww," said Johnny Parker. "Ain't they cute. The fuck are they?"

"Dunno," Henry said. "What's it called? They're made of paper. Ori…orig…origami or something," he said.

"What're they doing under there?"

"Fucked if I know," said Henry. He stood up, brushed his hands off on his jeans. "Weird."

"Yeah. Let's go," Johnny Parker said, already starting to walk away, toward Grafton Street.

"Yeah, okay." He looked at the animals one more time, shivered again suddenly, violently, and shook his head.

"Fucking weather," Henry groaned. He caught up to Johnny Parker and slugged his upper arm. "Booze Barn," he shouted, in a semblance of happy yelling.

"DUDE," Johnny Parker hooted, giving Henry a short shove. In this way, they made their way off to the bar.

. . .

Nathan hid behind the bushes till the loud guys moved on. It was awful when they spotted his animals, though he'd hoped one of the guys might at least know what they were for, that in such an accidental way Nathan might find out what he was supposed to use them for, or make of them, or do with them. But no luck. They were origami; sure, Nathan already knew that. The question was why were they being sent to the library? Even better, who was doing the sending? He was just going to have to be patient, he thought, and wait for it to become clear. He hated to think of them being stolen by someone while he paced the path. Because what if it turned out you needed to have all of them all together to get it, whatever it was you were supposed to get? He shuffled over to the clearing under the shrub where the animals sat. He liked being able to see them any time he wanted, but obviously, that just wasn't going to do any longer. He had trouble these days actually using his fingers, maybe from the cold. But if he concentrated really hard, he found he could move small items just by thinking about it. He focused on the origami for a while and managed to nudge them further under the bushes, to a more protected spot. Then he curled up in the bushes himself. It was cold and damp but he didn't mind. He closed his eyes and tried to think of Rebecca, but he could only see Leah. Seeing her made him feel bad, but he didn't know why. So he kept his eyes open instead.

. . .

Leah lay in the dark in her room; eyes wide open, staring at the ceiling. Wasn't much to look at up there, and she'd already counted the ceiling tiles. And here she was, still awake. She let out a lungful of breath. This middle of the night wakefulness was what she got, she supposed, for sleeping all day and doing nothing to earn a night of rest. Lying on the couch reading home decorating magazines wasn't exactly the kind of thing that could wear a girl out. It was plenty depressing, sure, and that brought with it its own kind of exhaustion, but it wasn't the kind that tended to lead to the satisfied, deep sleep she was craving. She wasn't going to find that kind tonight. She rolled over and looked at the clock. Coming up on two in the morning. God. Way too early to actually get up. Too late to get dressed again and pretend she'd just been napping. Way too late to call anyone, even Charlotte. Well, she thought, I can always get up and do the dishes.

"Yes," she said aloud. "I'll get up."

She sat up, gingerly put her feet on the cold wooden floor. The birds shifted in their cages. Neil sat up, too, and said "Biiirrrrit?"

"I'm getting up, Neil. Can't sleep. Downstairs?"

Neil stretched and leapt nimbly off the bed. On the floor, he stretched again, one leg and then the other, and looked at her intently while he did so.

"Don't get any big ideas, though," she cautioned him. "It's the middle of the night, which is no known feline feeding time. So that's not what this is about, as long as were both crystal clear, okay?"

Neil butted his head against her calf.

"I'm not kidding," she told him. She pulled her bathrobe from the chair beside her bed, and drew it on, knotting it at the waist. "Shall we?" she asked. Neil trotted out ahead of her and four-legged it down the stairs. Watching his furry butt descend, she was filled with nameless, wordless, inexplicable affection. How could such an annoying creature fill her with so much love, she wondered. It was such pure emotion, what she felt for him. And he was just a cat. His fur smelled like corn, his nails were sharp, he had a pesky way of standing on her lungs when she was trying to sleep, and he could not be convinced to stay off the goddamn kitchen counters. More than once she'd found his teeth marks in the butter. She wasn't even sure she really liked cats all that much, but Neil? Neil she loved. And these days, she was gladder than ever to have him around. This self-imposed exile needed company of some kind, and Neil's was perfect. She could talk or not talk and it was all the same to him. She never had to explain herself or apologise for her mood. As long as she kept the crunchies and fresh water coming, Neil was satisfied. And he made a comforting lump in the bed at night.

She moved through the house in the dark, the rooms barely illuminated by light from the street. Everything was different at night. The possessions she knew and loved so well were shadowy, their use inscrutable, their shapes even a bit sinister. She felt a tingle of fear as she passed by the basement door, enough to make her hurry her pace to the kitchen, where she fumbled to turn the light on quickly, to banish that prickle, keep it in its place in the dark. That was the deal. No scariness allowed once the lights were on. She wasn't sure who exactly she had this deal with, but she'd relied on it since childhood. The fluorescent lights of the kitchen were soothing to her now, and she brought her breathing back to normal. She surveyed the situation.

Pots and pans from the day's cooking were stacked haphazardly beside the sink, along with the side-plates and chevre-encrusted knives that were the detritus of Leah's usual spartan cheese-and-cracker meals these days.

She plugged the sink and ran hot water into it. A squirt of dishwashing liquid resulted in almost instant bubbles, and she began loading in the dirty glasses, plates and cutlery.

Leah loved to wash dishes. It satisfied the part of her that longed to take people and things that were fucked up, and make them whole and right. Doing the dishes was a particularly instantaneous way to gratify that desire. She loved to let her hands swim through hot soapy water. She loved the way the glass went all squeaky when it was clean, the way plates once dull could be made to gleam. She loved to return cutlery to its formerly sparkling self. She didn't like drying quite as much, but on a night like this, even the lesser of the two tasks could scratch her itch. She gloried in the clean stack of cups and dishes, the points of the knives seeming to glow in the bright kitchen. When she was done washing, she let out the water and decided to scrub the sink. The cleanser smelled bleachy and good as she sprinkled it onto the stainless steel. She scrubbed at the metal and felt a kind of pride in how clean she was making it. Even though it hadn't looked dirty, as she swirled clean water into the sink, washing the cleanser down the drain, the basin was notice-ably brighter. Leah saw what she'd done and decided it was good. She leaned back against the stove and felt calm.

She wished she had a cigarette. Smoking used to punctu-ate her days, signalling an end to every task, the beginning of another. But she'd had to give up when Nathan got sick. It seemed too willfully stupid to keep smoking when he had cancer, even though the kind he had had nothing to do with smoking. Nothing to do with anything, as far as they'd been able to work out. It was just cruel and unusual punishment for—for what? For nothing. What had Nathan ever done to anybody? Sure, he was a pain in the ass older brother, but what older brother wasn't? And she was sure he'd crossed a few people in his time, but come on. In terms of big sins? There just weren't any; that she knew of. She'd seen him fight with Rebecca, but what could you expect? They were both totally stubborn. Of course they fought. Didn't mean they didn't love each other, weren't perfect for each other. The whole thing just beggared belief, but if she started down that road, Leah thought, she'd never get off it. She'd never, ever again get to sleep. Better simply to lose herself in whatever she could. In this case, on this night, that'd be scotch and housework. She moved to the hoosier, took down the bottle of scotch and a clean glass. Poured the drink, not worrying this time about adding ice. She took the first warming sip, then pulled a tea towel from the drawer, put the drink aside, and began to wipe the dishes dry, one at a time.

. . .

Henry leaned over the bar and shouted "two tequila and orange juice" to the bartender, but he might as well have been whispering. She looked at him and shrugged, her beautiful naked shoulders rising and falling like a wave he could drown in. He wanted to put his lips right against her ear, talk right into her, and given the chance, he wouldn't waste his breath ordering drinks, oh no. But there was no way he'd be making time with this girl. She was way too beautiful, and besides, she was already irritated with him. He gave up on the mixed drinks, held up two fingers and yelled, "Two Keith's." She understood that one alright, turned away from him in a flounce of hair and breast and perfume—he swore he could smell it rising above the sweaty, smoky crowd—and bent to the beer fridge. He admired her perfect ass in its perfect low-rise jeans, each cheek lovingly outlined by the clinging denim. He felt the blood pounding in his head and in his pants and forced himself to imagine the machinations that would be involved in getting a girl like that to go home with him. Hell, in getting a girl like that to talk to him beyond telling him how much he owed for the two beers. That straightened him out pretty fast. It was an impossible situation, and he was already in one of those. No need to further complicate his deal. By the time she whirled around again, two cold and sweating bottles in her hand, he was over her. Or, more properly, he was over the moment of weakness that had let him think he would ever be in a position, ever be a lucky enough bastard that he would get the chance to get over someone like her. Hell, he couldn't even get over Tina, and it had already been almost a month since she'd kicked his sorry ass to the curb.

God, Tina. He grabbed the beers from the beautiful barkeep and took a long swallow out of one of them. She snickered in disgust. "Eight bucks," she yelled over the throbbing dance music. "It's eight bucks." He remembered himself, and grabbed for his wallet, his upper lip wet with perspiration and beer. He pulled out a five and a handful of loonies and pushed them toward her. Then he grabbed the beers again, treated himself to another long swallow, and pushed off to find Johnny Parker.

The night Tina kicked him out it snowed like a bastard. And she had really kicked him out. None of this nice breaking up you hear so much about, where you talk for hours and hours trying to settle your differences, and when it becomes clear that you just don't want the same thing, you both cry, and you hold each other, and then you climb into bed for some intense farewell sex, and in the morning you start looking for an apartment. And you live together civilly, even having more sex on occasion, if that's what seems appropriate, until you find a new place to live, and you remain friends and have joint custody of the cat. None of that for his Tina. Oh no. She sent him out in a hail of broken crockery, in a shower of shouted insults, in a barrage of sneered accusations. There was no soft sentiment in that breakup that was certain. He went down under her violence and he was still waiting to surface.

And sure, he wasn't blameless. Sure, he'd egged her on, he hadn't listened to her half the time she'd bitched at him for whatever it was he was doing wrong. But he never thought it would come to this. Come to him rootless, owning not much more than the pile of clothes currently mouldering on James and Emily's bathroom floor and the guitar that never dealt a harsh or unkind word his way. Come to him not even having a permanent place to live, for chrissakes, but shacked up instead in James and Emily's place while James was away on tour, dealing with signs of happy coupledom wherever he looked—the matching night stands in the bedroom, framed photos of the two of them throughout the house, their left behind toothbrushes leaning together in the glass on the bathroom shelf. There he was every day, taking in their mail, seeing none of his own. He was sure Tina was dumping his in a snowbank or burning it on the barbecue—she probably wouldn't even bring it in the house and burn it properly, in the fireplace—she hated him that much.

He couldn't figure it out. She was the one who had cheated on him. After all that time, and all her fear, and all her misguided accusations, in the end, it was she who could not be true. Henry had had plenty of opportunity, and had been plenty tempted. And to him it would have been just sex. But the thought of it made Tina insane, and he loved her, or thought he should, and so he never strayed. And finally, one night when he was in Moncton pinch-hitting for Johnny Parker in some Tragically Hip tribute band, Tina stepped out on him. When he got home, she was sitting there, thin-lipped, white-cheeked and she told him. Told him she'd slept with her art teacher, a great poncey old man she seemed to think was brilliance incarnate. And when Henry just nodded and sank down heavily into a kitchen chair and shook his head once or twice silently, she lost it. She started yelling and screaming and throwing things. She pulled him to his feet and hammered on his chest and raved at him, as if he were the one who had sold their relationship out. He took it, he took it all, and he never said a word. What was there to say? His silence only enraged her and she stood there in the kitchen, eyes awash in hatred and something else, something Henry couldn't place—disgust, maybe or despair—and she said in a voice so quiet that he almost didn't hear it: "I think you'd better go. I think you'd better get your fucking stuff and get out of my sight." Henry started toward the bedroom without a word, but Tina got in front of him and he reared back, as if she were on fire. "On second thought," she said evenly, "just get the fuck out now. You can come and get your stuff tomorrow when I'm at work, but if you don't leave right now, I think we'll both be sorry."

He could see she wasn't fucking around, so he groped for his coat as quietly and subtly as he could, as if any sudden move could make her explode again. He carried it in one hand; it hung down like the carcass of an animal he'd found in the woods. He looked longingly at his guitar as he passed it in the hallway, but he didn't dare grab for it. He could feel Tina's eyes on him from the kitchen, and for the first time in the five years he'd known her, he felt afraid. Real fear. And real pity, and a blend of other emotions with a rank bouquet, a blend he decided then and there to try as hard as he could to forget.

He took his leather jacket and let himself out into the night, then slid into its sleeves and zipped it up. He stood on South Street and wondered what the fuck to do. He went to the pay phone across the street and rang up Johnny Parker.

He moved now through the crowd at the Booze Barn, a crowd that seemed to undulate with one mind, or, more properly, he thought, with one crotch. He held the beers aloft and looked for Johnny Parker in the fray. Finally he saw him, his friend's six-foot-four frame towering above a group of—what else?—pretty girls. Johnny's blond curls were like a beacon in that room, and girls were floating his way, dashing themselves on his rocks. He leaned down conspiratorially and flirted with three girls who were probably in first year pharmacy, or maybe kinesiology. There was a sameness about girls like that, and on nights such as these, Henry thought, it's a sameness that comforts to no end. He came up on the group and handed Johnny Parker the Keith's he hadn't started to drink. They clinked bottles and Johnny Parker smiled a half smile at Henry, who raised his eyebrows back. The girls tossed their hair and Henry could feel them evaluating him. He did a mental inventory; did he feel air on his cock, meaning his zipper was down? Could he feel anything hanging out of his nose? When was the last time he'd actually seen his hair? And could they tell he really, really didn't care which one of them he went home with, as long as he went home with one of them? Did it matter if they could tell? Probably not. In fact, it would probably help. Oh, sure, they'd make it difficult for him, there'd be a hint of humiliation in it, but he realised he actually didn't give a fuck, as long as he could find himself, within a few hours, being led up the stairs to some two-bedroom flat, having to be quiet so as not to wake the roommate, snickering quietly and pushing his hands up some accommodating girl's sweater, as long as he could peel her clothes off and shed his own like a skin he'd grown out of, as long as he could climb atop some living, breathing, laughing, fucking girl and just move. That's all. Just move on her, move in her, move her, move the bed. As long as he could fuck and fuck until she cried out and then he did, until he could collapse, sweaty, spent, satisfied and fall into sleep and forget for a few miserable hours just who he was and how things had gone so very very wrong for him. Was it too much to ask one of these pretty young girls to take him home and let him disappear from himself for awhile?

Sometimes, Henry worried himself. Tonight, however, he was determined to ignore the nagging feeling that he was becoming deeply weird. He smiled at the brown-haired girl Johnny didn't have an arm around and said, "Wanna dance?"

. . .

Charlotte leaned back, her elbows propping her up against the bar.

"Can I buy you a drink?" asked the guy in the chequered shirt who'd been staring at her ever since her neat dismount from the mechanical bull. She'd landed on her feet in a cloud of straw on the floor, wiped her palms on her jeans, let out a lungful of breath and sauntered coolly across the room. The guy, however, had not been quite as cool. Now he was standing in front of her, nervous and red-faced. Charlotte looked him up and down. He wasn't exactly setting her on fire, but she was willing to try anything once. "Sure. Jack Daniels, neat," she said, twisting over her shoulder to deliver her order to the barkeep.

"Jack Daniels, neat," the nervous guy repeated. He swallowed hard. "Make that two." .

Charlotte barely tipped her cowboy hat in his direction, smiled at him with her mouth.

"Come here often?" the guy asked. At least he was consistent in his approach, Charlotte thought.

"No," she told him. "Never, in fact."

The bartender set two glasses up on the bar, poured the shots, said to the nervous guy, "Six bucks."

The guy pulled out his money, slid it across the bar. He handed a glass to Charlotte, kept the other one for himself.

"L'chaim," Charlotte said, raising her glass a moment.

"Gezundheit."

She laughed once, while confusion rippled across his face. She knocked the JD back and wiped her mouth with the back of her hand.

Nervous Guy took a big gulp of his drink, coughed and sputtered.

"Need a pat?" Charlotte asked, lifting her arm.

He flinched away then remembered himself, coughed and sputtered anew, and finally said, "No, no, I'm good. I'm good."

"Good," Charlotte said. She twisted over her shoulder again, held up her empty glass, caught the barkeep's eye, and said, "'Nother one, please." She looked at Nervous Guy. "You?"

He gestured to his drink, barely depleted. "No, uh, no thanks. I'm uh—"

"Good?" Charlotte said.

"Yeah," Nervous Guy said, nervously. "I'm good."

. . .

Henry wrapped his left arm around the girl—what was her name again? Amanda? Alicia? Alison? Fuck, he'd forgotten her name already. No, no, he had it. It was Amanda. Amanda kiss'n'hug, he thought, and laughed into her hair.

"What?" she shouted, over the pounding music.

"What?" he shouted back.

She shrugged her shoulders at him, raised her eyebrows.

"I couldn't hear you," he yelled.

She smiled up at him, squirmed a little in his arms. He smiled back. Who cares about conversation, he thought, when you've got a smiley, squirmy girl in your arms. He looked over at Johnny Parker who was making the two blondes laugh and toss their hair. Maybe it was going to be a good night. Maybe it already was.

. . .

Leah put the last of the clean glasses back into the hoosier. She sank into the rocking chair and wondered if she felt tired enough to sleep. Neil came padding into the kitchen stopped in front of her and meowed. "Hey bubba," she said. She leaned down to scratch the top of his head. He liked a good hard head scratching that cat. He purred a guttural purr, his ears flattening out to either side of his head. She bent down in the chair, hooked her hands under his armpits and lifted Neil onto her lap. He squirmed a bit, but when she went back to scratching his head, he smoothed himself out and submitted to being a lap cat, his little cat lips stretched around his little cat teeth in a rictus of pleasure, a Cheshire Cat grin.

Maybe this was the closest Leah would get to the perfect man she'd been promised by Psychic Sue. The perfect man who was supposedly just around the corner with his Cheshire Cat grin ready to give Leah everything she'd ever wanted. Psychic Sue had pestered Leah for years. Sue wanted to read Leah but something about Sue gave Leah the willies. Sometimes, when they ran into each other at, say, the flea market or out for brunch, Sue would let slip something she'd intuited about Leah's life or motivations or personality, and it seemed so invasive and show-offy. Sue was intense in a beyond-disarming way, and Leah could barely meet her eyes in public; she shuddered to think what it would be like when it was just the two of them alone in a room together, Sue focusing, psychically, on Leah.

And then Nathan died, and six months later, whipsawed by confusion, Leah called Sue and begged her to come over. She just couldn't stand it anymore, the wondering and not knowing, the lack of any reliable non-extra-sensory authority. And so Psychic Sue came. She set up a little alarm clock on the kitchen table, and asked for a piece of Leah's jewelry. Leah handed over the ring her parents had given her when she graduated from high school, a chunky silver band with cut out suns and moons, engraved with the words *carpe diem*. In the lamplight, Sue had offered a vision of the afterlife as a health spa, where all Leah's dearly departed hung out together by the pool, having raucous family get-togethers with good Italian food, playing Rummoli far into the night. The specifics were perhaps not quite so detailed, now that Leah thought about it. But Sue had told her that Nathan had had to recover when he got there—that he was sick when admitted to the afterlife, but that the attendants were able to do what their earthly counterparts had been unable to—they'd somehow stopped the rot that had eaten Nathan to death in this world, leaving him whole and healed and gloriously able to stay up all night, plate of cannolis at his elbow, steadily losing his heavenly pennies to his fellow dead, but feeling much better, thanks. Their grandfather's bone cancer in permanent remission, their grandmother's too-big heart beating on track again, their aunt's MS-shaking hands able once again to hold a flourish of cards, to deftly flick pennies onto the mat, their other grandfather's litany of complaints—what had he died of, in the end?—now all meliorated.

Leah didn't ask questions about this, because she couldn't think of what to ask. This seemed as reasonable a vision of heaven as any she'd ever had in her head, from her earliest understanding of angels as pudgy babies with wings made of white feathers, to her fervent hope that once she brooked those pearly gates herself, she'd be privy to all the information that eluded her on earth, like how to solve math problems, with trains departing Montréal and Winnipeg and meeting somewhere around London, Ontario, and whether she should have kept dating Timothy, who always made her take her shoes off soon as she set foot inside his apartment, and who never called her anything but dear, which was entirely too avuncular an endearment to be sexy. Of course, it'd be too late then for that kind of information to be much help. But she was looking forward to the hindsight part of it, at least.

Psychic Sue's answer about Nathan placated her for a while. It was, after all, the best one she had. As if to prove her point that Nathan was healthy now and happy, Sue passed along nagging messages from him. Don't wear so much black, especially close to your face; go swimming as often as you can; don't be afraid to scream; sing more; get back to making art the way you used to; stop drinking that brown stuff, it's bad for you; eat more orange food, orange foods are good; read more Faulkner; re-read *The Little Prince* before Christmas.

It was a strange list, not all of which made sense. She rarely had occasion to scream and it was winter, so swimming was a toughie. She thought about Faulkner a lot, but found the memory of him sufficiently inscrutable to keep her from trying to read him again.

But one day, in the second hand bookshop a few blocks from her house, she found a copy of *The Little Prince*, all out of order in the stacks. It seemed like a sign, and when she took it to the counter to pay for it, JW, the kindly owner, who always had a bit of sandwich in his beard, said, "Oh, you should just take that. Don't worry."

And so she did. She nodded mutely, put her crumpled five-dollar bill back in her pocket, and slipped the slim paperback in after. She walked home in a daze, walked directly to the bathroom, closed the door with a deliberate click though she was alone in the house, sat down on the floor and began to cry great sobs that wracked her, that made her worry she wouldn't be able to stop, that the deep sadness she felt would overwhelm her, overpower her, sweep her—and everyone she loved—out into a hot and salty sea.

She read the book one night when sleep eluded her. She read it avidly, eagerly, attentively. If there was a message there for her, beyond the one that was there for everyone, if there was something there for her alone, for Leah from Nathan, she didn't see it. She wanted to, desperately, but she just didn't.

And now, from time to time on nights like this, nights when sleep once again played hard to get, Leah sat in the kitchen, Neil on her lap, and tried to think just what the message might be. She rocked and scratched and wondered and thought. The night wore on.

· · ·

Charlotte finished another drink, put the empty glass on the bar decisively. "Well, Nervous Guy," she said, as Nervous Guy's jaw dropped open, "I've gotta ride on outta here. Been nice talking to you." She tipped her hat once more, turned on her heel and sashayed out of the bar.

· · ·

Amanda ground her pelvis into Henry's. Across the dance floor, Johnny Parker looked up from a sea of blondes and gave Henry a smiling thumbs-up. Henry swallowed the despair that was beginning to rise in his throat, smiled back at Johnny Parker and returned Amanda's pressure. She looked up at him through her bangs with a look that made

Henry's heart flip. No, to be accurate, it made his stomach swoop. Okay, to be truly honestly honest, he thought, it made his cock swell. Or maybe it was the grinding of her pelvis that was doing that. Either way, Henry thought, it's now or never.

He leaned down so his mouth was just beside Amanda's ear. Her hair smelled like flowers. He breathed in as if it was oxygen. He didn't know what he'd done to deserve this, though he could hear Johnny Parker's drunken voice in his head telling him it was his birthright, it was what he was en-titled to as a young, good-looking, single, guitar-playing god. He wouldn't believe it if Johnny Parker actually said it, and he sure wasn't about to take it from the voice in his head, but Henry was past caring what he'd done to deserve what he was about to receive. He cared only about receiving it.

"Wanna go?" he breathed into Amanda's ear.

"What?" she yelled.

Henry sighed, but was undeterred. "Wanna go?" he asked, louder this time.

"What?" she yelled again.

He stepped back from her ear, made eye contact. "Go," he yelled. "Let's go!"

"Oh," she said, surprised. "Oh, okay. Let me tell my friends." She looked over at Johnny Parker and his blondes. "Cherry!" she yelled. "Tina! I'm going!" She pointed at Henry, whose heart—no mistaking it this time, it was definitely his heart—dropped like an elevator free of its cables. Tina, Tina, Tina. Why couldn't she have been named Emintrude or Aloysius or some rare name he'd never heard? Those two syllables, the first creased his mouth into a smile, the last left his lips wanting hers. And where was Tina this fine night? Who was she making smile, whose lips were hers gracing? He felt that in his stomach, that was certain. He felt it like ice in his bowels. Her limbs, golden, all tangled up with some old codger's. Her hair on the pillow, flaxen, mixed with obscene grey. Jesus Christ. He closed his eyes. He staggered.

"Whoops, baby, watch out," Amanda said, putting out a hand to steady him. She gripped his left buttock, squeezed. She grinned up at him, her blue eyes depthless, her lips pink and chapped.

Henry steadied himself, shook off her hand. "Okay," he said, "I'm okay."

Amanda pouted at him. "Your place?" he said, in a conciliatory tone.

"Yeah," she said. "Looks like my roommates won't be home for awhile," she gestured to the blondes.

"Okay," Henry said. "So. Let's go." He put his hand on Amanda's back, felt her muscles flutter under his fingers, remembered what he was about. He steered her off the dance floor, to the door, and out to the street, where he gallantly opened the door of a waiting taxi and guided her inside. He climbed in next to her, put his arm around her shoulder, drew her close.

"Where to?" the cabbie asked. He had a long, dirty white beard and smelled of cabbage.

"Seymour Street," Amanda said, leaning her head on Henry's shoulder.

See, he thought, this is nice. This is nice, human interaction. This is what's been missing from my life, he thought, this kind of nice, human interaction. He pressed his lips to Amanda's hair, let his hand creep down to her breast, cupped it, lingered there. She brought her hand up to his, rested it, her fingers lining up with his.

The cab lurched forward, flinging them toward the plastic

shield that divided front seat from back. "Whoa, buddy," Henry said, bracing himself against the shield, one arm still around Amanda. "You okay?" he said to her. She nodded.

The cabbie grunted and gave the car a bit more gas. He drove with utterly straight arms; seat maximally pushed back, arms relentlessly straight, hands gripping the wheel rigidly at twelve and two. Henry looked at Amanda, rolled his eyes. She giggled and snuggled into him a little closer. He leaned down toward her till he could feel her breath on his face.

"What do you think would happen if I kissed you?" he asked.

She giggled again and said, "I don't know."

"Want to find out?" he asked, lips just centimetres from hers.

She nodded and her lips parted slightly. He pressed his to hers, extended his tongue, felt hers extend to meet him. As the cab raced through the streets of Halifax, Henry explored Amanda's mouth with his own. He probed beneath her jacket, finding her breasts again, inside her shirt this time, squeezing, fondling, rubbing. She let her hand fall into his lap, where his cock sprang up to meet it. He wished she'd move her hand around a little, but it just sat there. Anyhow, it was more action than he'd had in months. When was the last time he'd had sex, even with Tina? He couldn't remember, and was damned if he would try to start now. He pushed Tina out of his thoughts, kissed Amanda a little more vigorously, brought both hands to bear on her breasts. At last, they were at her house. He shoved a handful of money at the cabbie, pulled Amanda from the cab, kissed her long and hard right there in the middle of Seymour Street.

"Patience, baby," she said, pulling away from him and

laughing. She dug through her jacket pockets for her keys. She pulled out a Mars Bar wrapper, a bus transfer, a handful of Kleenex, some quarters, her driver's license, her student card. She did not, however, pull out her keys.

"Shit," she said.

"What's that, love?" Henry asked.

"Forgot my fucking keys," she said, patting herself all over again. "Shit goddamn."

"Isn't there anyone home?" he asked. Then he remembered. The roommates were with Johnny Parker.

"We can go to my place," Henry said doubtfully, picturing the mound of clothes on the bathroom floor, the dank sheets on the bed, the inhospitable, to say the least, kitchen. But if he kept the lights off, maybe it could work.

But Amanda was having none of it. "No," she said, "forget it. It's not worth it."

"What?" Henry said, sure he must have misheard her. Sure it couldn't have been as bad as it sounded. Turned out, it was considerably worse.

"No," said Amanda, "forget it. I'll just go sleep at my boyfriend's."

"Your *what*?" Henry sputtered. "Your boyfriend? What the fuck are you doing with a boyfriend?"

Amanda looked at him coolly. "The usual stuff," she said, "movies, dinners, long walks in the park."

"Yeah," Henry said, "but, okay, then, what the fuck are you doing with me?"

"Well, nothing," Amanda said pragmatically. "If I hadn't locked my keys inside, maybe, but, you know—"

"Jesus Christ," Henry moaned. "Jesus fuck," he continued.

"Okay then," Amanda said, "I've gotta go. I'll see you around. Take care, Harvey."

She walked away, a bit drunkenly, hips swaying, knee-high black boots kicking through the snow.

"It's Henry," he called after her. "My name's Henry."

"Whatever," she called back, not even looking over her shoulder. She disappeared down Seymour Street, while Henry stood in the snow, cursing.

. . .

Nathan couldn't sleep. More and more these days, he was having trouble drifting off. It was no good, he'd discovered, to think about Rebecca, no good to wonder how his parents were, to wish Leah would pop by for a visit. It didn't make him feel better, and as a matter of fact it made him feel a good deal worse. Instead, he thought about math. He'd always found his comfort in the ordered march of numbers, theorems, formulae. He sat in the bushes outside the main branch library on Spring Garden Road in the dead of night, and thought about Pythagoras and his theorem: Pythagoras Theorem asserts that for a right triangle with short sides of length a and b and a long side of length c, $a2 + b2 = c2$. He thought about all the times he'd used Pythagorean theory to figure stuff out—not just pure math stuff, either. Once he'd used it with his dad to help put the legs on a round tabletop Leah had found years ago and dragged home to furnish her first apartment. She was impressed and proud, he remembered, smiling, watching as he drew triangles and arrows and did computations on the underside of the big circle. He drew his knees up to his chest and leaned his chin on the platform his knees made. He pictured himself back in that kitchen. They were so young then, totally unformed. Her biggest fear had been that gravity would stop working.

His had been that he'd never fall in love. And look at them now, he thought. And then he burst into tears.

· · ·

Charlotte flagged a cab. "Windsor Street," she said, climbing inside.

"Right," said the cabbie, his long dirty white beard waggling. Charlotte sank back into the seat and started laughing.

· · ·

It was a long, miserable walk home. Henry jammed his hands into his pockets and felt sorry for himself. Fucking women. Unfuckingtrustworthy women. The wind whistled over the Common and parted his hair. He felt kicked, that was all there was to it. It wasn't Amanda, of course. Who cared about her? It was everything. His fucking songs, his fucking life, his fucking undone laundry. And Tina, Tina, always Tina. Jesus. His guts roiled, twisted, bucked and turned. It took his breath away, it really did, the thought of her, the way she used to fold herself into him in bed at night, the way she looked in the morning, all sleepy and dear, the way she'd looked that night in the kitchen, the way she'd looked at him. The way she looked in his imagination, astride some grizzled artist, head thrown back in ecstasy, the way it rarely had been for him in recent years, her tender throat bared, her tiny perfect breasts bobbing on a sea of beauty. It was too much. Too much entirely. He sank down in the snow, put his head in his hands and cried.

· · ·

Leah hugged Neil hard enough to make him squeak. Maybe now, she thought. Maybe now I'll be able to sleep. It was nearly three thirty. Another couple of hours the sky would begin to brighten, and then it'd all be over. She pinched the skin and fur at Neil's neck once more then dumped him gently to the linoleum. She got to her feet and thought for a moment about pouring a nightcap but decided against it and drew herself a big glass of water instead. The water splashed against the clean sink, glistening in the lamplight. "Night Neil," she said, taking up the glass of water and clicking off the lamp atop the hoosier. She flicked off the overhead light as well, and started down the dark hall to the stairs.

· · ·

Henry pulled himself to his feet, disgusted. With himself, with Amanda, with Tina, with the whole sorry night. The snow had soaked through his jeans and left him wishing he'd worn those dank underwear after all. He stumbled out of the Common, across the street, and down the one block to James and Emily's. Turned the key in the lock, the handle on the door and fell into the house. "Thank Christ," he said. He shed his jacket in one motion and took the first stair in the next. On the other side of the wall, he heard his footsteps matched. "Too much booze, fuck," he muttered. At last he gained the upper floor, made it to the bedroom, peeled off his clothes and fell into bed and fast asleep.

· · ·

The birds stirred as she entered the room, but she whispered *shhh*, though she was sure it made no difference. There was her dear looking little nest of a bed, the hollow where her body had been still carved out. She slid out of her bathrobe and beneath the duvet, closed her eyes and sighed, waiting for sleep to come again at last.

. . .

Charlotte placed her cowboy hat on the dresser, smiled at herself in the mirror, whispered *yeehaw* to her reflection, and went to wash her face.

. . .

Johnny Parker couldn't decide who he liked better, Cherry or Tina, and just when it looked like they'd all go home together, all drunk and horny, Cherry and Tina started making out with each other and completely ignoring him. He walked home across the frozen Common alternately cursing his luck and fantasising about what Cherry and Tina would do when they got home. All in all, he thought, not a bad night.

. . .

Henry awoke with a mouth like a swamp and a head stuffed with cotton. He groaned and rolled over, away from the light streaming in through the window. "Last night," he said aloud to no one in an attempt to remember how he'd ended up so miserable. It came back in flashes. The Pool House, the library, the Booze Barn, Tina. Wait, was that right? Had he seen Tina last night? Jesus Christ! He sat up, too quickly, and felt his vision darken at the sides. He let out a long breath and lay back down. No, not Tina. A brown-haired girl, though, with a boyfriend. "Jeeeeessssuuuuuusssssss," he moaned, rubbing a hand over his face. He shook his head. It was behind him now, though, and no better place for it.

He had to make a change, he knew. Had to stop screwing around, had to get serious about himself, about his life.

"You can't go on getting drunk and picking up college girls in bars," he said sternly to himself in the stillness of the room.

"Wait a minute," he answered himself, "why can't I?"

That was a puzzler. He waited, and thought, but no reason presented itself. Still, he didn't feel particularly good today, and that was a direct result of having got terribly drunk last night and picking up a college girl in a bar. So, no more. At least for the time being.

And more than that, he was going to get healthy. He was going to get out of bed right now, this second, and go for a run. Yep, that's right, a run. That felt good, that felt right. That felt like the opposite of the previous night's debauchery and dissolution. He sat up, swung his feet down to the floor, stood up. He stretched, arms to the ceiling, squinting in the sunlight.

In the bathroom, he rooted for some running clothes. Sweatpants and a long sleeved shirt, again the problem of socks. The hairdryer had been a neat trick, so he turned that on again, blew fresh a pair of grey gym socks and pulled them on.

Back in the bedroom, he pulled the sheets off the bed, surprising himself. He stripped the pillows of their cases, and shoved the sheets in one, took the other to the bathroom and pushed his dirty clothes inside it. He twisted the tops closed, then jogged down the stairs, full of virtue, to the basement. Detergent, hot water, the machine began to fill, and he dumped the clothes in. Extra detergent, maybe. It'd been a while. Even Henry didn't know exactly how long. He closed the lid on the washer, jogged back up the stairs.

In the kitchen, he pulled open the fridge, surveyed its contents. Three kinds of mustard. An assortment of mostly empty jam jars. Two beers, a bottle of soda water that had been in the house at least as long as he had and was no doubt by now flat. Yogurt containers that also predated Henry, and that might or might not contain what their outsides advertised.

"Right," he said. "This is disgusting. So, no breakfast, okay, I'll run to the store."

And feeling like he had a mission, Henry sprinted to the living room to stretch his legs.

. . .

Leah selected a piece of hot pink paper from the origami packet on the kitchen counter. She pictured Nathan, and as always, the first image she got was of him sick, in the hospital, his feet grotesquely swollen, alarming, greyish-green. She wished it was otherwise, but she always saw him this way first. She struggled past that and tried to picture him well and walking, but the best she was left with today was a vague impression of the way his body moved through the air, the angle at which he stood, the way his hands made loose fists to keep his arms from flapping. Her mouth twisted to the side as she thought of him, and she bent her head to the paper and composed the day's message: *A feeling of relief,* she wrote, *in the quiet room. The heat subsides.*

She folded the square into a dog and took it back upstairs to Harold.

"Your turn," she said cheerily, reaching into the cage. Harold was bright-eyed this morning, and the feathers on his head were ruffled again. She felt a wave of affection for the creature. He was almost cute. She attached the paper dog to his sheath, patted down his head feathers, and carried him over to the window. She held him tight in one hand and raised the sash with the other, then took him in both hands, stretched her arms out the window and tossed him up into the air.

"Hurry back," she called after him. "And bring me something, why don't you?"

. . .

Henry heard the woman's voice as he began to jog down Moran toward the Common. He turned to see her, but he could see nothing but brilliant sun. The voice was unfamiliar, and as far as Henry knew, he knew no one on the street. He stopped running and stood still, looking back the way he'd come. There was no one else out, no one on the sidewalk, no one starting a car, no one locking a front door. The woman had clearly been talking to him, but who the hell was she and why would she call after him? It was, to be sure, a puzzle. And then out of nowhere came a rush of wind, the flapping of wings. "Fucking bird!" Henry yelled, for the second time in as many days. It was a greyish-brown pigeon, same as the other had been, though this one had something bright pink attached to its leg. It seemed to throw a look at him before it took off again, swooping over the Common. Henry shook his head, trying to shake it off, and started running again. He thought for a moment about following the bird, but his stomach gurgled and he remembered his mission. He curved away from the bird and ran across the Common toward Quinpool Road.

In the grocery store, Henry pushed the cart through the brightly lit aisles. He leaned against it, glad of the chance to catch his breath. He really hadn't run very far, or very fast, but he was winded. He really would have to quit smoking again. And actually, it shouldn't be that hard, he thought, considering how broke he was and how much cigarettes cost. Still, he had run. And he felt incredibly virtuous about that. It filled him with inspiration as he strolled through the produce aisles leaning on his cart like an old man leaning on a walker.

Filled with new appreciation for his health, he loaded fruits and vegetables into the cart, added a loaf of multi-grain bread and a box of frozen tuna steaks. He grabbed yogurt, granola, extra-pulp orange juice and free-range eggs. In the pharmacy aisle, he picked up all-natural tooth-paste and deodorant, and a twelve-pack of toilet paper just for good measure. He backtracked to the health food sec-tion for a block of tofu and a box of veggie burgers. He was browsing the wheat-free cookies when he heard her voice. Tina. Goddamn. He could feel his face flush to the roots of his hair. She was talking loudly to someone who wasn't talking back, he thought, but that didn't seem right. She came around the aisle and opened the freezer door, shifting the cartons of soy-based ice cream substitutes. She held a shiny silver cell phone squeezed between her ear and her shoulder, and she was talking into it.

"Carob Mint," she said, loudly, as if to a screaming toddler. "You like that, don't you?" Henry couldn't hear the response. He shrank behind a display of kamut pasta and watched her through the packages. She leaned right into the freezer case so her ass was in the air, and still her voice boomed out. "Strawberry Ripple?" she said. "De-alcoholised Rum Butter?" She went quiet for a minute. Henry knew he should just keep backing away, back all the way to the cash register, pay for his groceries and get the hell out, run all the way home, but he was caught in a death-grip of fascination. He hadn't seen Tina since the night she'd thrown him out, and now here she was, rampaging through the grocery store like an ill-behaved soccer mom. Where on earth had that cell phone come from? And who was she talking to? Henry couldn't figure it out. Maybe her nieces had come to visit, or maybe she was talking to the child of a friend, but it didn't add up somehow.

"Rene," she said—that's when it hit him—"Rene, sweetie, I can only tell you what flavours they have. I can't bring you home Cookies'n'Creme if all they have is Carob Mint, baby, you dig?"

Now Henry could hear the other voice, though not what it was saying. Rene the cranky old artist was yelling at Tina, as she stood buried to the shoulders in her grocer's freezer. He was yelling at her, apparently, about flavours of ice cream. And Tina, his Tina, his fearless, take no shit, give-back-at-least-as-good-as-you-get Tina, was standing there, hands turning white in the frigid air, taking it.

Henry smiled broadly, turned his cart around and headed confidently for the checkout.

At the checkout, he scrabbled through his wallet for enough money to pay the bill. He was going to have to find work soon; these healthy groceries did not come cheap. And they weren't exactly light, either. Once they were bagged, Henry finally realised the folly of his plan to run to the grocery store—there was no way he could run back with all those bags. Even walking would be a chore. Fuck it, Henry thought, it won't cost more than five bucks to take a cab, and I can go for another run later on. Meantime, though, his stomach was bitching that it hadn't eaten a square meal since at least yesterday, maybe longer. And Henry was itching to get back home to his guitar and see about beating his head against that brick wall for a few hours. It was a day for getting things done, and if that meant spending a few bucks on a cab, well, so be it. He gathered the bags, staggering a little under their weight, and wobbled to the cab-stand to see about getting home.

. . .

In the study, Leah nudged the computer on. She'd made tasting notes on the few bites of soufflé she'd been able to manage, and she had a few thoughts on the cookie recipe, too. She needed to write them up while they were still fresh in her mind, and send them off to her editor at *Bite This*, the cooking magazine she worked for. She'd been letting this part of her job slide a little, and that wouldn't do. It was one thing to cook and create, but if she didn't keep Laurie apprised of her progress, she wouldn't get paid and if she didn't get paid, well, she'd have to get a real job, and that might prove difficult, what with her reluctance to leave the house, and all.

She was tired of herself, anyhow, tired of thinking about herself, feeling sorry for herself. Tired of wondering where Nathan was and tired, so tired, of feeling guilty, both for cutting him loose and for everything before that. She needed the pure, unbiased immersion of a morning's work to bring her back to the world.

That, she figured, and anything like a sign from Nathan. But at the very least, the work.

The computer booted up slowly, and Leah stared out the window. The maple tree in the backyard reached its grey-brown fingers to the sky, a sky the same colour as the tree itself. The snow in the backyard beyond her fence was trampled down, rolled into balls, tinted with food colouring, hollowed out, all at the whim of the children who lived there. It drove Leah crazy to see it. Winter drove her a bit crazy. The only time she liked it was after a snowfall when everything was fresh and white, untouched, clean and new. Strangely, she also loved the spring, when all was mud and chaos. It was these last days of winter that wore her down though. And this trouble with Nathan wasn't helping.

She wondered how he was making out. It was funny, she realised, she had no idea what his needs were, whether he knew he was missing, whether he missed her. She missed him. No question. Even though having him around spooked her.

He had revealed himself to her slowly, over several months. He never said anything to her, but he turned up often, stood by and simply stared at her. It didn't seem to matter where she was, or what she was doing. More often than not, she'd catch a glimpse of him, fleeting or otherwise. It started at the library.

She'd been asked to write a piece for *Bite This* about the last dinner on the Titanic. It seemed like a somewhat ghoulish idea to her, but she had to admit she liked the idea of salmon mousseline and roast loins of one kind of meat or another.

She'd spent the day at the library, researching the wrecked ship. It had been a trying day, all that freezing cold water, all those high waves, all those devastated families, those lungs filled to overflowing with saltwater, those blue fingers clutching stricken throats. She'd had to wade through pages and pages of heartbreak to find any mention of the food. It hadn't been a priority, it turned out, for many of the authors who'd written about the doomed voyage. She was exhausted by lunchtime, and it really wasn't helping that Nathan was standing there, just standing there every time she looked up from a page or computer screen. He wasn't exactly looking at her, but he wasn't not looking at her. And it had startled her every time.

By now she was used to seeing, about once a week, someone who looked like him. Someone she'd almost swear was him. When that happened, she'd think, well THERE you are, for chrissakes, where have you been? It would take her a moment to realise, and then her mouth would go small, lips pulled inside it as the wave washed over her. With astonishing regularity she saw him. The Chinese Nathan driving an SUV, something the real Nathan would never have done. The black Nathan pushing her kids in a shopping cart through the Superstore. The blond Nathan running down a field after a frisbee, shouting at his teammates to get the lead out. So many Nathans, and never the same one twice. But this, in the library, this was different. This was Nathan. Nathan Nathan. And it was completely unnerving.

He didn't look the way he did when he came to her in dreams, and that was a good goddamn thing. Because in the dreams—well, at first, in the early days, he'd clearly been dead. That is to say, he'd been a corpse. Or, more properly, he'd been a zombie. In one memorable dream that came maybe two weeks after the funeral, Nathan had pursued her around some suburban ranch-style house on a gurney. He was just skeleton in places, his mouth hung open and reeked of the grave, his eyes were hollowed out and eternally staring. And he wanted her brain. To eat. It would have been comical, if it hadn't been horrifying. It would have been comical if Nathan had still been alive and she could have called him up the next day and said, "Dude, last night, in my dream, you were a zombie piloting a gurney expertly through this ridiculously large, nice house neither of us lived in, and I was running away from you because you wanted to eat my brains!" And Nathan would make some crack about how she must have been dreaming because he was by far the smarter one and had no use whatsoever for her brain. And she'd have laughed and told him to fuck off, and he'd have laughed and asked her when she was coming for a visit, and they would have made some vague plans to see each other.

But instead, she awoke alone and sweating, shivering, in the middle of the night, too terrified to move an arm outside the blanket to turn on the light, lest some wayward zombie sink his teeth into her soft, live flesh. She awoke too guilty about the fear and revulsion she'd felt towards him in the dream to feel okay about feeling scared awake. She awoke too miserable to feel sorry for herself. And then that passed and she did feel sorry for herself. She felt plenty sorry for herself, and sorry for him too, and she hoped he wasn't a zombie, doomed and damned to wander in search of comestible human brains, and then she remembered he'd been cremated and was just ashes now and a bone fragment or two and maybe a silver filling. And he was in a vase in a glass case in Hamilton, Ontario, and not on a gurney, not in a suburban ranch-style house, not anywhere. Unless she believed Psychic Sue, in which case he was behind her left shoulder most of the time, but that didn't seem right either, because wouldn't he just hang out with Rebecca instead? Why her? Psychic Sue was obviously not to be trusted, she was obviously just telling her what she wanted to hear, because if Psychic Sue actually knew what she was about, then where was her man, goddamnit? Where, for once and for all, was her Cheshire Cat grinning man, the man of her putative dreams, picket fence, dog, kids and all?

In any event Nathan had continued to appear to her in dreams. After a month or two, he morphed from a zombie into merely a dead person. In one such appearance, he took her for a ride beneath the stars in his go-kart, and when it was time to go, he said, "I'm going to teach you some math, now," and Leah looked at him steadily while he unscrewed the top of his head, then unscrewed the top of hers, tilted over her and poured pink and purple and blue numbers from his skull into hers. "Thanks," she said, before climbing out of the go-kart and watching it ascend, Nathan aboard, to the stars. "Thanks," she called, waving after it.

In each subsequent dream, he became less dead. Once he rescued her from a malevolent water park and told her things he knew about her own strength and resilience that brought her to tears, tears that were still on her cheeks when she awoke. She lay in the stillness for some time that night, touching the tears on her cheeks and willing him to come back, to come back to her when she was awake. But she knew, at the heart of it, that she was a little afraid of him, too. After all, he was a ghost.

He didn't appear to her. Not that night. And not for many nights to come. He came in dreams, with the usual frequency, and each time he got healthier looking. With the exception of the water park dream, he'd always show up in some kind of wheeled cart, most recently a hay wagon. He was the most like a live person in that dream. Dressed all in black, and refusing to make eye contact, and, frankly, a bit crabby, but in the dream, she believed he was alive. She knew he was special in some way, troubled in some way, but she also knew he was in the world. She hadn't seen him be that way, a participant in the world, since six months before his death. She woke up feeling joy, and that's when she saw him. He was sitting in the chair beside her bed watching her.

She tried to scream, but couldn't, as if she were still sleeping. She managed a kind of strangled cry, but he sat impassively. He flickered in and out, as if he were a radio with bad reception, but it was him for sure. Not because it looked like him, necessarily, Leah would explain, or try to explain, to Charlotte later that day, but just because it WAS him. She couldn't be clearer about it. Just, she knew it was Nathan, she knew he was there, she knew it was for real.

And after that, he was always with her. At first, having him around was great. Leah felt like she could take incredible chances, and Nathan would look out for her. It was a feeling she had of invincibility and divine intervention in her stupid, messy life. She tested this feeling by stepping into the road without looking both ways, and was exhilarated when cars screeched to a halt for her. Charlotte pointed out that this was likely because she lived in Halifax, where drivers would stop if a pedestrian so much as looked at the curb, and not because her dead brother was watching over her. But Charlotte was occasionally tediously attached to empirical evidence, as Leah did not hesitate to point out, and Charlotte was hard pressed to argue with her on that front.

Most of the time, Nathan kept to himself. She couldn't always see him, but she had a sense that he was there. And most of the time, she found it comforting. She experimented a little with talking to him, but she wasn't sure what she should tell him or what he'd want to know. She'd asked him things occasionally, like why he was with her and not at home with Rebecca, but Nathan would flicker out under questioning, and Leah didn't like to upset him, so mostly she didn't say anything.

She thought about explaining where her head had been those last six months he'd been alive, but every time she tried to tell him, it came out wrong. Nathan would just hold his hands up in front of him each time another of her ham-fisted explanations started. He'd hold his hands up and look away, look down, off to the side. It was disconcerting. Leah remembered reading somewhere that if you were visited by a ghost and you wanted them to leave, you just held your hands up and said, *no*. That's what it looked like Nathan was doing. It was upsetting for both of them, and eventually, she stopped trying.

Her failure ate away at her though, in a way it hadn't before he'd started hanging around her. She did her best to put it out of her mind, but she could feel him standing behind her, or moving around her almost all the time, and it was difficult to forget something that had proved to be so formative. It was starting to make her edgy, keeping it inside, but eventually Leah got busy with more recipe work, and that made it easier to forget what she was convinced she had to forget.

And then, his presence was upsetting in other ways. She could feel him tensing up every time she drank a cup of coffee even though she'd switched to decaf after her visit from Psychic Sue. She bought sweet potatoes and left them under the counter till they smelled like vodka. Then she'd put them in the compost, go to the grocery store and buy more. She wore black turtlenecks in spite of him, but every time she did, she felt cross and out of sorts for no good reason.

She'd start to masturbate, then imagine him on the chair beside her bed and stop short, too ashamed to carry on.

"And god forbid I should bring anyone home," she bitched to Charlotte on the phone one day. "I mean, how can I? How can I have sex in my room while my dead brother watches?"

"Hmmm, that's a toughie," Charlotte said. "Honestly, I don't know what to tell you about that one, except that, oh, he's a ghost, and you're alive, and sweetheart, a woman has needs, you know what I'm saying?"

"Yeah, I know what you're saying," Leah said, twisting the cord around her finger till the flesh at the fingertip went white. "I'm too guilty to masturbate, remember?"

"It's not perfect," Charlotte admitted. "But what are you going to do?"

"Excellent question," Leah said. "I wish I knew."

The next day, at the library, Leah put aside her research on Indian cookery. She leaned back in her chair and sighed. The library was usually a refuge for her. She easily lost herself there in the lemony smell of well-thumbed paper and the murmuring of street kids warming up in the magazine room. But she couldn't concentrate. She had Nathan on her mind.

She got up from her chair, leaving her stack of books, her fine tipped sharpie, her notebook. The various tools of her trade. Her scarf hung on the back of her chair, a deflated, forgotten streamer. At the computer terminal she hesitated for just a minute, her fingers itching over the keyboard. It wasn't logical, what she was about to do. And yet, what choice did she have? She looked furtively over each shoulder. And then she typed "ghosts."

The screen filled with titles. Kids' books, volumes of maritime ghost stories, something called "Ghost of a Chance," which seemed to be a romance novel with a paranormal twist. Leah refined her search. *Ghosts, nonfiction*, she typed. *Dealing with them.*

This time, there were fewer titles. She scratched down the call numbers of a few on a scrap of paper, cleared the computer screen and went into the stacks to take a look.

The first one she put her hands on was a fat hardcover with no dustjacket. The spine was green, with black letters. "How To Deal With Ghosts."

"That's to the point." Leah muttered as she drew it from the shelf. The pages inside were buttery soft, polished by hands and time.

How To Deal With Ghosts, the title page read, *by Peter Pietropaulo*. The chapters were equally straightforward. *What are ghosts*; *Why do they stay on earth*; *How do I know if I have a ghost*; *How can I get rid of my ghost*; *What if I decide I want my ghost back?*

Energy can be neither created nor destroyed, she read. *And so it stands to reason that when we die, our energy remains. And sometimes, that energy takes a ghostly human form. Sometimes we actually see spirits; they appear as flickering, thinner versions of themselves. Other times, we may simply feel their presence—a cold or hot spot in a room. We may hear spirits knocking or wailing. Some spirits manifest as an odour. Roses, sulphur, chicken soup, coffee. Lights may flicker. Appliances may turn on or turn off, on their own. We will discuss these symptoms of a haunting in depth in the chapter entitled "How do I know if I have a ghost?"*

"No mystery there," she said. "I definitely have a ghost. I'd say seeing him is a pretty clear symptom." An old man who was browsing in the stacks gave her a dirty look and held his finger up to his mouth. "Sorry," she whispered, then rolled her eyes when he turned away.

She hurried back to her seat with the book. Her stack of cookbooks sat naggingly beside her notes. She had a deadline she'd already pushed three times. She cracked the cover of "How To Deal With Ghosts" and spent just enough time reading it to formulate a plan. At five o'clock, before Joan shooed her out and locked the doors behind her, she borrowed the book and stowed it in her bag, alongside her recipe notes, her plan for freeing Nathan humming in her mind as she rushed from the library.

"I have to tell Nathan his story," she told Charlotte over a very spicy caesar at the Fish Tank.

"Surely to god he knows his own story," Charlotte said. "He's a ghost for the love of Mike, don't they have access to everything?"

"Not according to this book," Leah said. "Not if they're just hanging around. It means they're a bit lost, a bit confused. I mean, if he were haunting his own house, that'd be understandable, you know? He should want to be close to Rebecca, he should want to watch over her. But he's thousands of kilometres off course even for that. Let alone for just settling easily into the afterlife."

"What about the all-night card parties?" Charlotte said, "what about the endless meatballs?"

Leah grimaced, sipped her drink. "Yeah. You know, I think I extrapolated that stuff."

"Extrapolated," Charlotte said, blinking. "You mean the pennies from heaven are not falling from some cosmic

Rummoli game?"

"Are you making fun of me now?" Leah asked. "I can never tell if you're fucking making fun of me." She turned on her high chair. "Can I get another drink?" she said to the passing barkeep. "I'm going to need at least another drink, here."

Nelson nodded and looked at Charlotte, who nodded back. "Yeah," she said, "looks like it's fixing to be a long night."

"Look," Leah said, as patiently as she could. "I don't know about the meatballs, okay? I don't know about the white clothes, and I don't know about the heavenly Rummoli game. I would like to think things work that way, but I can't be certain. When I really think about it, I'm pretty sure all Psychic Sue told me was that when he got there he was sick, and they looked after him till he got better."

"Who're they?" Charlotte asked, slurping caesar through a straw. She coughed. "Gah. Spicy."

"I don't know who they are. Could be my grandparents and my aunt Mary, could be angelic paramedics, could be God himself for that matter. Sue didn't elaborate and I didn't ask. She did say Mary came to get him, because my grandmother was getting things ready. I took that to mean meatballs and Rummoli. I don't think that's out of line, frankly, and I have to say, it's an image I like. So, I don't know. If that's what the afterlife was like and I had the option, that's where I'd stay, especially if my grandmother was doing the cooking."

"Maybe Nathan didn't have the option."

"Maybe not indeed," Leah said. "This is what I'm thinking."

"Why don't you just ask him?" Charlotte asked.

Leah shook her head. "Nah, he doesn't really like

questions. He puts his hands up like I'm the paparazzi or something."

Charlotte hooted. She looked around. "Is he here now?"

"You gotta quit it with that," Leah said, shaking her head.

"Come on, Leah. Just tell me, is he here right now?"

Leah took a deep breath, tilted her head down, looked at her friend from under her eyebrows. "Charlotte," she said.

"Just tell me, and then I won't ask anymore."

"He's not a puppy, Charlotte, chrissakes, have a little respect."

"I do, dude," Charlotte said. "I have plenty of respect. But frankly, if I'm going to listen to anymore talk about how you can't even jerk off in case your ghost is watching, well, I'm going to want some payback. So is he here or isn't he?"

Leah laughed, looked over her shoulder. "He's sitting back there," she said, jerking her thumb toward the empty stools at the bar. "And he doesn't look happy."

Charlotte took a long swallow, traced letters on the table in the condensation her glass left there. "Do you think he ever fucks shit up?" she asked.

"Fucks shit up?" Leah repeated. "You've gotta be kidding."

"No," Charlotte said, her face a model of sincerity. "Really. Like, do you think he uses his ghostly status to check out naked chicks or steal money or eat cake?"

Leah rubbed her hand across her face, hard. "No, I don't think he checks out naked chicks or steals money or eats cake. Charlotte, he's a frigging ghost, first of all. No corporeal body, you dig? What would he do with money, or cake, for that matter? Or naked chicks? And second of all, you never met Nathan, but he was ridiculously law abiding. Steal cake, for godsake."

"I would steal cake," Charlotte said.

"Yes," Leah said. "Yes, Charlotte, I imagine you would steal cake. Nathan, however —"

Charlotte looked right into Leah's eyes, raised her eyebrows. Leah sighed.

"Okay, yes, he does fuck some shit up. He moves my keys. He took my iron and kept it till I ran out of clothes I could wear without ironing, waited till I bought a new one, then gave the old one back. He occasionally takes photos of nothing with my camera. Like photos of light, or of the cat a split second after he's left the room, or of, I don't know, dust motes, or who knows, other ghosts. One day he moved around all my plants, I don't know why. No reason, I'm sure."

Charlotte chewed her straw. "Does it bother you," she asked.

"A little," Leah said. "A little bit I wish he'd leave me alone, a little bit I feel honoured that he chose me to harass." She smiled a half smile, looked over her shoulder. "But mostly I just worry about him. Mostly, I just wish he'd figure himself out and move on, you know?"

"So," Charlotte said. "What're you gonna do?"

"Well," Leah said, straightening up in her chair, "I'm going to try telling Nathan his story."

"How much do you figure he needs to know?" Charlotte asked.

"Dunno," Leah said. "Right now, I'm thinking he needs to hear the whole thing, from the time he kind of stopped living in the world, to the time he stopped, well, living."

"Whoa," Charlotte said.

"Yeah," Leah agreed. They sat in silence and worked on their drinks.

"So how do you do that?"

"Not sure," Leah said. "I guess I just kind of have to start.

He's not crazy about direct contact, you know? He's kind of sketchy, never looks right at me, that kind of thing, so I think I have to just, I don't know, kind of talk out loud to him around the house. I mean, I already talk to Neil all the time, so hey, why not talk to the ghost of my brother, as well, you know?"

"No," Charlotte said, "I don't. But it sounds like as good a plan as any. Want another drink?"

"Yeah, oh yeah," Leah said. She looked over her shoulder and signalled to Nelson. And noticed that Nathan was gone.

But that wasn't the night he went for good. He took off now and again, and Leah wasn't sure why, or where he went. It was possible, she imagined, that she just lost her ability to see him once in awhile, but she had never been able to work out a pattern, why he was visible to her one minute and not the next. It had never worried her much when he'd disappeared in the past, but the night he took off for good was different. She'd known it that night, known he hadn't just gone for a stroll.

She sighed as she sat there in front of the computer. That night had definitely been different, and she'd wished, time and again since then that she could simply delete all that had gone on. The way she'd talked to Nathan and the chill she'd felt the next morning when she realised he was gone for good. She put her head down on the desk and tried to picture him at the library, receiving her latest missive. She imagined him unfolding the dog, smoothing out the creases, reading the words written there in thick pencil, understanding them as another link in his chain.

. . .

The morning rush of walkers and buses had mostly cleared out, and Nathan emerged from the bushes. He felt prickly, strange, maybe from being so confined all night. He thought he'd take a stroll through the library, get out of the damp for awhile. Though it hadn't bothered him much in recent days, he thought perhaps it was now the cause of his unease. He took the steps carefully, protecting his sore body, and waited till a woman in a puffy ski jacket opened the library door, then scooched in after her. He forgot all about the birds as he wandered the stacks, his long fingers tracing the spines of hardcover books wrapped in clear plastic. He loved the crackly sound they made, the surprise of soft pages, the detritus of other readers. A stray hair, a bit of orange pith, a grease stain from some long-ago eaten snack, pages turned down to mark a place forever. He looked at the titles and the authors' names as he trailed his finger along each shelf. A person could read a book every day their whole life and still never really make a dent, he thought.

. . .

Henry paid the cabbie with the last of his cash, and struggled to the door with his groceries. He wiggled the key in the lock and finally got the door open—he would have to talk to James about that, he thought. Or you could try to fix it yourself, said a voice in his head and so astonished was he that he turned to see where it had come from. All these voices all of a sudden! Maybe he was finally freaking out. But no, on sober reflection, he recognised the voice as his father's, and quickly dismissed it. He didn't have time to fuck around with the lock. He had songs to write. And groceries to put away. And clothes in the washing machine, he remembered. He ferried the groceries to the kitchen and got them mostly put away, the perishables, anyhow, the dry goods it didn't matter as much, he'd get to them later. He took the basement stairs two at a time, moved the clothes from the washer to the dryer, and put in his second load. Here he was, getting things done. Tina could go fuck herself, and so could his dad, for that matter, and just for good measure. He was making a change, he thought. For once and for all, making a change.

It felt good to make a decision. He pushed the start button on the dryer, remembered fabric softener at the last minute, opened the door, threw a sheet in, and started the mechanism again. Happy, with the smell of Bounce on his fingertips, he vaulted back up the stairs to the kitchen. He fixed himself a bowl of organic yogurt topped with granola and a sliced banana, poured a huge glass of juice and ate standing up, looking out the window at the backyard. He swore he could feel health returning to every cell with each bite he took. He swore he could feel the hydration expanding his brain with every sip of juice. He swore he was making a change for once and for all, for good. Committing to himself. He was going to run every morning. And every evening. Sure, why not? He was going to eat right, three times a day, maybe more if the running made him really hungry. He was going to quit smoking, as soon as he was done the pack still crumpled in the pocket of his leather jacket. And most of all, he was going to get upstairs and write the hell out of those songs. He downed the rest of the juice and headed purposefully up to James's music room.

At the top of the stairs, he paused. Maybe he should take a shower. He was kind of sweaty from the run and the shopping, and he reeked of smoke from his night in the bars. He caught his reflection in the mirror. Also, he was wearing fucking sweatpants. Thank god Tina had been too involved in her soy ice cream to notice him at the grocery store. It galled him to think of her pitying him because of his attire. She would think the sweatpants were an admission of failure, of a basic inability to carry on in society. But some people, he thought, his colour rising, some people actually take care of themselves! Some people run to the store for exercise. Well, fuck her. She hadn't seen him, and anyhow, it didn't matter. But he didn't think he'd be able to write in sweatpants. He had to admit; they did feel like giving up. If only it were warmer, he could wear shorts to run in. Maybe James had some of those high-tech spandex running tights. Though those left nothing to the imagination, at least they looked like the kind of pants a person who cared about himself might wear running.

Henry stripped off the offending garments as he moved down the hall to James and Emily's room. He rifled through the dresser drawers, but James didn't have any fancy running duds at all. And all of Henry's clothes were in the wash. He felt very strongly, however, that he simply could not write if he was dressed like a bum. It just didn't go with his new approach to his life and work. He rifled through James's dresser again, this time looking for serious writing clothes. He found a pair of sharp black pants, the kind of pants that really should be worn with underwear. Well, fine, Henry thought. The wash would soon be done, and in the meantime, he could take a shower. He opened the closet and pawed through the clothes neatly hung in there till he found a crisply ironed purple shirt.

"Excellent," he said aloud. He padded to the bathroom naked and ran water for his shower. It came out freezing cold, and refused to get any warmer. Fucking hot water tank, he thought, twisting the tap off. I'll have to wait for it to fill. He padded back to the bedroom and perched on the edge of the bed. He dug through the pockets of his jacket, which he scooped off the floor and replaced on the chair by the bed, for his cigarettes. He opened the pack. Four left. He might as well smoke them while he waited for the water tank to fill up again. Get them over with. Make the shower the start of his new way of doing things. Out with the old and smoky, in with the new and healthy, he thought, striking a match. He took a deep drag on the cigarette, leaned his back against the wall and drew his knees up to his chest.

. . .

Johnny Parker woke up feeling like shit. He reached for the glass of water on his nightstand, but it was empty. He smacked his lips together, thought, what the hell, rolled over and went right back to sleep.

. . .

There was a kid in the library Nathan felt sorry for. He saw the kid hanging around a lot, gangly in a big parka. He seemed like a nice, polite kid, and he was around even when the weather was really, really bad, so probably, Nathan thought, the kid was genuinely homeless. The bird trusted him, too. Nathan often saw the bird go right to the kid in the parka. He'd take the plump body in his hands, remove the little coloured paper animal from its leg, then hide it away in the bushes with the others. Nathan didn't know why the kid did this—he never seemed to care much about them, or even look at them again. And if he knew that Nathan was spending time hanging out with the paper menagerie, he didn't seem to mind. He was gentle with the bird, too, though he wasn't affectionate toward it. For affection, the bird came to Nathan. Once the kid had removed the origami shape, hidden it and moved on his way, the bird would hop-fly to Nathan and just hang out with him for a bit. Nathan came to think of the bird as his because of this.

And he became fond of the kid in the parka, too. He thought he'd like to help the kid, but frankly, Nathan wasn't really sure how to do that. He was pretty sure he'd had an idea at one point, but that notion, like so many other notions, was just a figment now, just a tingle on the tip of Nathan's tongue. The kid was skulking around the stacks in his giant parka, and the library ladies clearly didn't like it. On the weekends, or at night, the kid could hang out till the doors closed. The staff at those times could easily have been his friends. Young kids, greasy hair, lots of piercings, and snarling faces. But during the weekdays, the library was staffed with upright, uptight ladies with sensible short hair or closely controlled buns, glasses on beaded chains that rested on their shelf-like bosoms, or scraggly chicken legs that poked out from beneath knee length skirts. They were parodies of themselves, Nathan thought, and they did not like the kid. On any given day they could be guaranteed to follow the kid around the library till they came up with some reason to run him out or till they got tired of following him and ran him out for no reason. This was one of those days.

"Come on, man," the kid said in his foghorn voice. "It's freezing out there."

"Too bad," said the librarian with the grey-red hair. "This isn't a homeless shelter or a high school, it's a library. You're bothering the other patrons, and you're going to have to move along."

Nathan knew it was unfair. The kid hadn't been doing anything. There were hardly any patrons, besides himself, and the kid wasn't bothering him. But Nathan was pretty sure the library lady wouldn't listen to him. No one at the library ever did. Frankly, the service there was terrible.

The kid moved toward the exit, his big sneakers clomping on the steps. Nathan hurried after him. If he'd finished law school, he thought, he could offer to help the kid. Maybe they could sue the library or at least that mean librarian. But he hadn't finished law school, and though he knew what was happening to the kid was unjust, he was too shy to approach him, too shy to offer his help. He slid out the door behind the kid and watched dumbly as the kid loped away down Grafton Street. He raised a hand in half salute, but the kid didn't look back, probably didn't even know he was there. Nathan might as well have been invisible.

. . .

Henry lit his third cigarette and wondered if the water tank was full yet. He'd check it after this cigarette, he thought, tilting his head back against the wall and drawing the smoke down into his lungs. He'd get started after this cigarette, for sure.

. . .

Leah leaned back in her desk chair and looked out the window. The sky was relentlessly grey, the light weak and unconvincing. It made her study a gloomy place, this one that once had been cosy. But now it was stuffed with remnants of the past. Clothes she didn't wear anymore but was too lazy to get rid of. Old school papers. Board games she'd forgotten how to play, and ones that hadn't been that interesting to begin with. Nathan's first guitar, its battered face splintered. His Hardy Boys books and her Nancy Drews, sharing shelf space and swapping dust motes. Leah felt hemmed in. The grey sky, the artifacts she never used and rarely really looked at, but somehow couldn't part with. The endless work of making food she didn't feel like eating. The futility of it all, of a grey day in late winter with no end in sight. Maybe this would be the year the end simply didn't come.

. . .

Henry smoked his fourth cigarette right down to the filter.

. . .

Nathan stood on the library steps and watched everyone in the world go about their business. Overhead, a grey and brown bird was flying in circles.

. . .

Leah took a break. She went downstairs and made a pot of tea.

. . .

Johnny Parker laughed in his sleep, rolled over, and slept some more.

. . .

The bird alit on the library steps and strutted around Nathan's feet.

"Hey fella," Nathan said. He crouched down and reached out toward the bird, which looked at him with one bright black eye, cocked its head and cooed. "C'mere," Nathan said, "It's okay." The bird took a tentative step toward Nathan. From its sheath dangled a bright, tattered creature.

"What happened, here, I wonder," Nathan said. It wasn't clear what this one was meant to be. Somewhere along the way, it got messed up. A dog maybe, though its leg looked broken. He looked around for the kid in the parka, but he was nowhere in sight.

"We should move over, little guy," Nathan said. "It's kind of busy here on the steps." The bird cocked its head; its black eye glinted. "Let's go check out Winston Churchill," Nathan said. He balled his hands into fists in preparation for a bout of pacing. The bird skittered along the path beside him. Nathan stood and looked at Winston for a while. He wished he knew what to do. Finally he decided he should do what he'd been doing. He should wait. Eventually, the parka kid would come back and take the new animal and put it with the others. In the meantime, Nathan and the bird would hang out. He started pacing the path.

The bird hopped about nearby, foraging in the snow for a snack, a dropped french fry maybe, or a bit of pizza crust. This was prime hunting ground for such morsels, Nathan knew. At night, the library path was trod by drunken fools carrying the last of a dripping donair, or the two-foot long crust from one of those ridiculously large slices of pizza. Large enough to serve as a cape, and certainly more than anyone could eat. But that didn't seem to stop the people staggering home, snacks in hand.

At times like that, Nathan made sure to press himself against the side of the building. Sometimes, if it was really busy, he'd go to his spot in the bushes, where he felt more protected. He didn't like to look at the people, so he usually kept his eyes closed. They were too drunk, their eyes were unpredictable, and they made fun of Winston Churchill. It was all too much for Nathan. But he was patient, and it passed, and then he had the library lawn to himself again, in the cold and the quiet. He might see a solitary straggler, but those didn't bother him, not the way the groups did, with their loudness and their energy and the feeling of imminent danger that hung around them like the smell off the harbour.

In fact, he felt sorry for the solitary stragglers. They always seemed so lost, like they'd become disconnected from the group and didn't know where to go anymore. They were like the bird that flew behind the V at harvest time, the one who broke formation, flapped out of time, forced to fly behind, always behind. He wondered if those birds ever made it, and what it was like for them when they got there. Did the other birds welcome the stragglers? Were they sorry they hadn't waited? Did they promise not to do it again? Nathan felt a stab of sorrow. He faltered in his step. The bird hopped closer to him, the battered pink dog dragging in the snow. Nathan closed his eyes, breathed, and started to pace again.

. . .

Henry was out of cigarettes. Time to see about the laundry, he thought. He pulled on his jogging pants again and went down to the basement to check the dryer. His clothes were fluffy and warm and inviting. He smiled to himself, satisfied, and pulled them from the dryer. One more load for the washer, he thought, and then I'm back in business. He made the switch, moving wet clothes from the washer to the dryer, adding the last batch of dirty duds to the washer, lots of soap, cold water this time, since he still had to take a shower. He twirled the knobs and pushed the buttons and when the machines were clanking and whirring, he took the armload of clean socks and underwear upstairs and laid it all neatly on his bed. He mated the socks and rolled them up together, folded the underwear and sheets. He buried his nose in the fragrant cleanness of his towel, carried it to the bathroom and turned on the shower. He stepped out of his pants and then stood beneath the spray and began to sing. He lathered his hair and rubbed it till he could hear it squeaking. He couldn't remember the last time he'd washed it actually. He pushed the bar of soap over his limbs and torso and felt glad. Life could be so simple, if you let it, he thought. When the water began running cold, he twisted the taps off and stepped out of the tub. Rubbed himself down with his clean, fluffy towel, returned to the bedroom and got dressed.

He almost cried at the feeling of clean, warm cotton against his ass. He pulled James's pants on over his own gitch, buttoned-up the purple shirt over his soapy smelling chest hair. He pulled on a clean pair of black socks, looked at himself in the mirror and said, "Hey there." He rubbed a little gel into his long hair, pulled it back with an elastic and thought, well, I am ready for just about anything. It seemed a shame to waste such a pulled together package on staying home, Henry thought. Maybe he'd just go down to the corner and get a pack of smokes. Yeah, that'd work. And then he'd come right home and get back to those songs.

He ran down the stairs, feeling full of purpose, shoved his feet into his boots, grabbed his coat off the newel post and was away.

. . .

Leah sipped her tea and looked out the living room window. She heard the door slam next door, and felt the accompanying reverberation. She scowled through the curtains at the guy who ran by—so that's who was doing that!—but he wasn't even looking her way. She made another mental note to email James in England about his house sitter, who was far and away the most inconsiderate neighbour Leah had ever had. She retied the belt on her bathrobe and thought about getting back to work. If she could get a good few hours behind her, then she could relax for a while, maybe call up Charlotte, see if she wanted to hang out. So it was back up the stairs to the study.

The wind howled at the old windows of her study, as if in a rage about being kept out. It was supposed to get much worse, the radio had said, and she was glad to be tucked away safe inside. Later, she'd make another pot of tea, and maybe figure out something else to bake, to fill the house again with warmth and comforting smells. But for now, the typing needed doing. Her tasting notes and recipe modifications still waited by the laptop. There wasn't much to this job of hers, she knew, not much of consequence. The world wouldn't stop turning if Leah Black could no longer test and refine recipes for *Bite This* magazine. She probably wouldn't save any lives with her work. And in fact, there was a good chance she was part of the problem. After all, she could be using her expertise to be part of the free-food collective that served vegetarian meals each week in front of the public library to whoever needed or wanted a bite. Instead, she wrote recipes that called for expensive ingredients and acres of time. Recipes and stories that appeared in a glossy upscale magazine, bought by people who had two healthy incomes, or those who fantasized about that kind of carefree life.

On the other hand, she believed she was helping make people happy. And surely there was nothing wrong with that? She sighed, and opened her notebook. There'd been a time when making a difference in the world had meant everything to her. And now all she did was make soufflés. "Still," she said to Neil, who curled on the floor by her feet. "Goddamn good soufflés, when it comes right down to it." He opened one eye, twitched an ear at her, and then rolled over and went back to sleep. Leah began to work.

. . .

Henry decided to go to Willie's. There was a closer corner store, but he didn't like the guy behind the counter. Sam. He always looked at Henry as if Henry were actually covered in dirt or something. He had a lot of nerve, that guy, considering his store was full of stock that had been hanging around since no later than 1982, and the shop windows were yellow with dirt and cigarette smoke, and plump fly carcasses lay upside down on the sill, their crinkled up legs curling toward each other. It was enough to make a person sick. That, plus the judgmental way Sam looked at him, talked to him. Henry didn't need to go through all that, just to buy a pack of smokes. So Willie's it was. Sure, it was a few blocks away, and the weather was starting to turn, but it was worth it, and besides, Henry was feeling great, all clean and presentable. It was nice to be outside actually looking like a contributing member of society. Maybe he'd run into Tina, even.

At Willie's, the bells chimed when he pushed the door open. The shop was full of neighbourhood types—old dudes Henry remembered all standing around smoking and talking to Willie, but rarely talking to each other. It made for a confusing cacophony some mornings. Three or four grizzled old dudes ignoring each other on the surface but paying enough attention to talk to Willie one at a time; to at least not talk over each other. The smell of old man overcoat was often stifling. On mornings like that, Henry would get his smokes and his bread and get out of there. But if the crowd of oldsters was small, Henry would linger for a while, looking at the magazines, browse the soups, stand in front of the cookies waiting for a craving to tell him what to do. Then he'd take his purchases to the counter and joke with Willie, or with one of his kids, the oldest boy behind the meat counter, usually the plump daughter with the incredible green-grey eyes behind the cash register, and Willie presiding over it all. On this day, the shop was at old man capacity, so Henry simply shouldered his way to the register, pulled out his wallet and asked for his smokes. It was the younger daughter today, the one who never said a word. She barely made eye contact. Henry wondered about her sometimes, wondered how she got along in such a robust yell-y family, wondered what would be the thing, finally, that would pull her out of herself, wondered if perhaps nothing ever would. She couldn't find the cigarettes Henry wanted, and though he tried to guide her—"Those ones, right there, the blue ones. No, to the left of those. No, not those ones, the mild ones. No, those are menthol"—it was no use. He was on the verge of hopping over the counter and grabbing them himself when the bells on the door jangled again, and the shop was filled with the unmistakable sound of Johnny Parker, fresh from sleep.

"Ho, boys," Johnny's voice gravelled. He cut through the crowd of old men, clapping them on their backs, setting off a symphony of old man catarrh. Amid the crust, and the throat clearing, Henry heard his friend greeting the oldsters. "Arnold, my man, good to see you man. Huey, still hanging in there, that's good to see old man, good to see." The crowd murmured and parted as Johnny Parker moved through it like a politician, till finally, he was at the counter.

"Henry," Johnny Parker said, holding out his hand, "put it there." Henry inserted his hand into the one offered, flashing for a moment on himself as just another old man in the corner store, so seamlessly did his name fit, so similar Johnny Parker's greeting. Henry disentangled his hand from Johnny Parker's, waved it helplessly toward the silent daughter still groping for his cigarettes.

"He'll take the same ones as me, lovey," Johnny Parker said smoothly. The silent daughter turned pink across the tops of her ears, reached for two packs of Johnny Parker's brand and slid them across the counter.

Outside, the two paused to peel open the wrapping and began to smoke. "What're you saying this fine morning, Henry, my friend?"

Henry drew a lungful of smoke into his body, and then coughed it out like a seventh grader.

"You okay, my man?" Johnny Parker asked in his old-man-at-the-corner-store voice. "You alright there?"

"Yeah, fine," Henry said, sputtering, his eyes watering. "I just remembered I wasn't going to smoke anymore as of this morning. Fuck, goddamn."

"I'll take them off your hands," Johnny said. "No problem, man."

"No, no," Henry said, with a vague wave. "I've started, I might as well finish."

Johnny Parker nodded. "Come upstairs?" he asked.

Henry thought of his guitar waiting for him at home, the clean sheets standing by to be put on the bed, the laundry in the washing machine, the clothes in the dryer.

"Sure," he said, "for a little while at least. Why not?"

An hour later, as he was rolling another joint, he yelled over the jam band pulsing out of the speakers, "So what happened with you and those girls last night, anyhow?"

"Mmm," Johnny Parker said, emerging from the kitchen with a litre of milk in one hand and a bag of oatmeal raisin cookies in the other. "Fuck dude, wasn't that set to be a party."

"Set to be," Henry said. "It sure looked like it. So what happened?"

"Girls started making out with each other, Jesus Christ," Johnny said, opening the milk and taking a long swig from the carton. "Want some?" he asked, proffering it to Henry.

"Yeah, uh, no," Henry said, "what the fuck happened after that? You get in there?"

"Naw," Johnny Parker said, grinning lopsidedly. He opened the bag of cookies, took out a handful. "Once they started in on each other, they forgot all about me. Totally ignored me. Went at each other right there on the goddamn dance floor. Nothing I could do about it, so I just went home, laughing all the way. You believe that?" Johnny

Parker shook his head, laughed. "How about you man, how'd you make out?"

Henry rolled his eyes, suddenly feeling better about his own fucked up night. "Mine had a boyfriend," Henry said. "She'd forgotten her keys or something and we couldn't get in to her apartment, so instead, she says, she might as well go sleep at her boyfriend's. Fucking believe that? Like, the only thing kept that guy from getting cheated on was that she was too dumb to remember her keys. Christ."

He held up the joint, squinted at it. "Gotta light?" he asked.

Johnny Parker pulled a zippo from his pocket, handed it over. Henry sparked it up, took a drag, lay back. "Fucking amazing music, this stuff," he said. "Got any of those cookies?"

It was late afternoon when Henry remembered the changes he had waiting for him back at James and Emily's. "Shit, dude," he said to Johnny Parker. "I gotta go. I got a bunch of stuff to do today, and it's getting late."

"Gig tomorrow night, remember," Johnny Parker said, unperturbed. "Wanna go out later?"

"Yeah, later. Give me a call or something," Henry said. He brushed the crumbs off James's pants, grabbed his jacket and lit out across the Common. Shit. He'd forgotten about that gig tomorrow night. He was totally behind.

THE WIND PICKED UP THE SNOW ON THE LIBRARY LAWN AND GENTLY BEGAN TOSSING IT AROUND. It rippled the bird's feathers, and parted Nathan's hair. People hurried in and out of the building, mostly out. It was getting late, and the sky was starting to darken. Soon, Nathan knew, the library would close, and things would quiet down. Already, the steps looked inviting again. He was tired of pacing, and the wind was making it all the harder.

"Come on," he said to the bird. He nodded his head toward the library steps. "Let's take a break."

The bird sailed across the library lawn at Nathan's knee height, then perched on the steps, waiting for Nathan to catch up. They sat together, and waited, a task at which Nathan was becoming very good.

"There you are," the parka-clad kid called as he raced along the path. "Thought I'd fucked it up. I totally forgot about you today."

Nathan shrugged. It wasn't the first time. He was surprised, though, that the kid was speaking to him. Why today of all days? And had they meant to meet? He couldn't remember. If they had arranged a meeting, it was news to him. Still, he stood up and extended his hand toward the kid, but the kid went right past him and picked up the bird. Of course, Nathan thought, the bird.

The parka kid grasped the bird's plump body in both his hands and said, "What happened here? Thing is all bashed up." He removed the little pink dog from the bird's leg. It had become even more tattered in the time the bird had spent pecking in the snow, and its little torso was beginning to unfurl. Nathan peered over the kid's shoulder.

There was something inside the little dog. Words written inside it. Nathan felt nervous, his mouth went dry.

"Hey!" the kid said. "What's all this?" He unfolded the animal and smoothed out the creases. "Damn," the kid said. Nathan leaned in closer for a look.

A feeling of relief, the pencilled words read, in the quiet room. The heat subsides.

Well what the hell did that mean? Nathan sat back on his heels. Was it for him? He had no idea.

"What the hell," the kid said. He looked at the bird. "Are they all like that?" The bird cocked its head to the right and opened its beak, as if to answer. The parka kid scrambled to his feet and said, "Wait here."

Nathan hugged himself. He felt excited and scared. He wondered who the message was for, himself or the kid. He wished he could ask, but the kid clearly didn't want to talk to Nathan. He didn't even look at him.

Putting the scrap of paper carefully in his pocket, the kid

sprinted to the bushes where he'd hidden the others. He hauled them out and took them back to the library step. "Are they all the same?" he asked the bird. "Do they all have messages inside?" He started to unwrap each one, carefully.

They reminded Nathan of fortune cookies, and of the first time he'd used chopsticks. Leah had come to visit him in Ottawa, and they'd gone out for dim sum on Sunday morning. He'd had trouble manoeuvring the food from his plate to his mouth, he'd get it precariously balanced between the ends of the chopsticks, but halfway to his mouth, it'd burst out and fall into his lap or back to the plate. Finally, halfway through the meal, when he was almost insane with hunger and frustration, Leah had noticed that he was holding the chopsticks the wrong way around.

"You're eating with the handles," she'd said, gesturing with her own sticks. "You want to use the thinner ends for picking stuff up, dude." He watched her use the slender points of her chopsticks to snag a dumpling from the bamboo steamer that sat between them, and expertly pilot it to her waiting tongue.

"Huh," he'd said, and tried it her way. She had been right.

The best part, though, was always the fortune cookies. Breaking them open, reading the messages inside, feeling thrilled at their accuracy or intrigued by their mystery. He regarded the paper menagerie spread out on the library step. His fingers itched to open them himself, but the kid had them all lined up.

What order had they arrived in? The kid couldn't remember now. He knew the blue one had come just before this latest pink one, so he unfolded that one first. It was a message about machines. But the others? He couldn't remember their order. Green, orange, gold, red. He unfolded them willy nilly and laid them out on the steps.

A long flight, only sorrow at the end, one said.

A gathering storm, you kept time with your breath, another pointed out.

The bell in the night calls us and we come.

The tether slips, you slide, you soar.

Well those didn't make any sense either, Nathan thought angrily.

"What the fuck is all this," the kid exclaimed. So he didn't know either, Nathan thought. The kid moved the slips of paper around, changed their order, but it didn't help. The wind winkled their corners, threatened to lift them, but the kid protected them with his body, made a shield against the coming storm.

Nathan leaned further over the kid's shoulder, and read the messages over and over. They reminded him of something though, there was a memory just outside his memory, of what these could mean. Was it just the fortune cookies he was thinking of, or was there something else as well? His memory had become so holey lately. He could barely remember his own name.

He sat on the steps in the wind, tucked right up against the parka kid, and together they read the messages again and again. The kid moved them around on the step, as if some new combination and permutation might cause the seismic shift that would unlock their secrets. Nathan's mind skipped over and around the phrases, The tether slips, you slide, you soar. He rolled it around in his mind. And finally, he remembered what it reminded him of. And he knew what he had to do.

. . .

Leah finished typing and sat back. It was so hard to get started lately, but so satisfying to finish, to have done more in a day than, well, than what she'd been doing lately. Lying on the couch, reading magazines and fretting. The wind was becoming more intense, shaking her little study and hammering at its single-glaze windows. She stretched and thought about soup. It seemed like a lot of work to make it just for herself. But maybe she could get a jump on her recipe work for the next issue. She stretched her arms up over her head. It had been a long afternoon of hunching over the laptop.

"Alright, time to get this stuff off," she said, to no one in particular. She typed a quick email to her editor and attached the document, and as she was about to press send, the lights went out.

"Shit," she said, as the darkness of the very late afternoon settled around her. She waited a beat. The lights went out pretty regularly, especially when the weather was rough. But just as often, they came on again after a minute or two. This time, though, the darkness persisted.

"Oh for crying out loud," she said. The gloom of the afternoon was gathering quickly, but she could still see to navigate past the bookcase without stubbing her toe, and past Nathan's guitar without knocking it over. She made her way down the stairs and stood in the dim front hall, wondering where the flashlight was. In the basement, maybe. In which case, that's where it would stay. The basement made Leah nervous at the best of times, even with all the lights on. In the darkness? There was no way. Candles would have to do. She moved to the mantle, which was crowded with candles of various heights and sizes. She pawed along the mantle till her hand brushed a book of matches. She lit each of the candles she found, then moved on to the kitchen and lit what candles she could find in there, too.

The phone rang. Charlotte. "The power out there, too?" Charlotte asked.

"Yep, I just finished lighting all the candles. It's actually kind of nice."

"How was your day?" Charlotte asked.

"Better," Leah said. "I worked, all day. Got stuff done. It felt really good."

"That's great," Charlotte said. "They're letting us out early. No power here, no work, you know?"

"Yeah," Leah said. "You should come by. We can eat cold soufflé if the power doesn't come back on."

"You got it," Charlotte said. "I'll be there in a flash."

Leah hugged herself and rubbed her upper arms with her opposite hands. The house would start to feel chilly soon, and if the power stayed out for long, she was going to need blankets and extra socks.

In the kitchen, she rooted around by candlelight in the dark refrigerator. There was soufflé. A little sunken now, and probably considerably tougher than it had been, but still, it would be tasty. And cheese and crackers, of course. And fixings for a spinach salad with strawberries and pecans she was about to work on. She pulled the food out and put it on the counter, then remembered the cookies. She took the plastic container from the freezer and set it on the table to thaw. Not a bad spread, she thought, all things considered. She began assembling the salad and contemplated what kind of dressing she could throw together for it.

In the silence of the house—no radio, no appliance hum

or furnace roar, she could hear rattling. Harold coming home, or tree branches brushing windows? She glanced at the clock. It was getting late. Past time for Harold to come back, actually.

She cocked her head and listened for the happy ruffling that would mean two birds in the house, but all she heard was the rattling that sounded, she decided, more like branches on glass than birds in cages. She grabbed a candle from the kitchen and went upstairs to check, just to be sure, but there was no Harold. She made a search of the upper floor, holding the candle high, but still, no sign of the bird. She went back into the bedroom, and saw it. The candle reflected in the glass. Fuck, she'd forgotten to open the window. She put the candle down and was about to lean on the sash when the doorbell rang. Charlotte.

. . .

Nathan stared hard at the paper messages. Maybe they weren't even for him, but they didn't seem to be for the kid in the parka either. But then why did the bird wait around? Why did the kid in the parka take the animals and hide them in the bushes? And why did the bird always seek out Nathan afterward? It was time to be bold, Nathan decided. He leaned against the kid in the parka. The wind whistled over them both and knocked the kid's hood back. Nathan put his mouth close to the kid's ear.

"Write back," Nathan said urgently. "You have to respond to those messages. Write. Back."

The kid bent at the elbow, shoved his hand down the back of his parka and scratched a spot on his shoulder. He sat back on his heels. "This is crazy," the kid said. "I don't make enough money for this. Nobody said anything about any messages."

"You have to write back," Nathan said again. He wasn't sure he was getting through to the kid, but he knew it was his only shot. "I'll tell you what to write."

The kid looked around for the little grey brown pigeon.

"Hey," he called, "birdie. Come on over here." The bird looked up from its pecking, so far fruitless, and hop-flew over to the steps.

"What's your game?" he asked the bird. "What the hell?" The bird cocked its head, the way it did, and blinked. "This is stupid," the kid said, finally. "Some kind of stupid joke. I don't need this bullshit. Haven't even seen my money, lately."

He started to get up. Nathan felt panic rising in him, swirling in his chest like the wind that lifted granules of snow on the library lawn. "Sit down, sit down," he cried. "Please, you have to listen to me."

The kid hesitated. Nathan reached out and grabbed the ragged hem of his dirty parka. He didn't want to, but he had no choice. He pulled the boy back down to seated.

"Just write," Nathan said. "It won't be that hard. It'll only take a minute. And once I get things figured out, I will get you some money, I promise. Just, please, please hold the pencil for me."

"You know what," the kid said to the bird, "two can play this game. Wait here." He hopped up again and pulled open the heavy wooden door of the library. A minute later, he was back, with a stubby pencil punctuated with bite marks and a slip of scrap paper from the library reference desk. He sat back down on the steps and thought.

Nathan sighed with relief, adding his breath to the wind that leaped and danced and battered against the kid's parka-clad back as he hunched over the messages. "Okay," Nathan said, right into the kid's ear. "Here's what you write. You write, I am here, where are you?"

The kid put the end of the pencil in his mouth, added to the bite marks already there. He said to the bird, "I should just write back something like, oh, very funny. Where's my money? Hey, that rhymes!"

The bird made a sharp, scolding sound in its throat, and closed its eyes for a moment. Then it hopped closer to the kid and stretched its beak toward the pencil.

"Hey," the kid said, lifting the pencil up. "Get lost."

Nathan leaned in again. "Listen to me," he said patiently, and with all the persuasiveness he would once have needed in a court of law, had things gone that way. "You must listen. You cannot believe how important this is. This is what you write. You write I am here, where are you? That's it, that's all you have to do. Write it. Just write it."

The kid sat on his heels. He chewed the pencil's end. He closed his eyes. He thought about his girlfriend and their stupid fight. He thought about his father, who didn't understand him, and his mother, who'd taken off and left him when he was in grade five. He thought about the library ladies, who'd scowled when they saw him duck in for a pencil and paper. He took a deep breath, and then he figured out what he really wanted to say.

At last he leaned down to the scrap paper and scratched out, I am here, where are you? He folded up the scrap, placed it carefully in the bird's message sheath, and took the pigeon in his hands. He spoke quietly to it, using an even voice and encouraging words. Then he held it aloft and bounced his arms up toward the heavens, and let the bird go in a volley of feathers. He visored his eyes with his hand, and watched the bird flap away, north, over the city.

Nathan sat back. Relief flooded his body. It would be only a matter of time, now. He let out a breath. The wind picked up at the same time and grabbed the unfolded sheets of brightly coloured origami paper. It lifted them up and for a moment they hung, suspended in front of the library doors while Nathan and the kid sat on their heels, mouths open. And then the wind just exploded, flinging snow and coloured paper like strange confetti over a stranger parade. Nathan put his arm around the boy's shoulders and drew him into the bushes, to the little windsheltered cove against the library's front wall to wait out the storm.

· · ·

At first, Henry thought it was just a random pigeon, though he'd never seen any hanging out in the street like this one was. As he got closer, he saw the bird had something attached to its leg. He kept an eye on it while he unlocked his door, in case the little fucker might try to dive-bomb him, the way it had the other day. He got the door open, and looked back at the bird. Suddenly, it winged toward him, and Henry let out a cry and ducked down, but this bird didn't try to take his head off. Instead, it flew inside the house, landed in the back hallway and stood there looking at Henry, black eyes glinting. Henry stood in the doorway, uncertain. "Come on, birdie," he said. "Come on out of there now." But the bird just looked at him, then turned and hopped toward the kitchen.

"Oh, come on, chrissakes," Henry said. He flicked the lightswitch in the hall, but nothing happened. "Naturally," he said. "Lightbulb must be burnt out." He crept down the hallway after the bird, not wanting to startle it or cause it to peck his eyes out. The front door hung open, and he half-hoped the bird might just turn around and fly on out. On the other hand, he was a little curious about the message on the bird's leg, and the thing did not seem inclined to leave. Maybe it was for him, the message.

"Don't be absurd," he chided himself aloud, but when he got into the kitchen, the bird was up on the counter, tamely awaiting him. He flicked the light switch on the kitchen wall and was only mildly surprised when nothing changed. "Power out," he said aloud. There was a flashlight, he remembered, on top of the fridge. He picked his way toward it through the bags of groceries still on the kitchen floor. "Sorry about the mess," he said lamely, before remembering he was only talking to a bird. He shook his head. Fucking Johnny Parker. He was too high to be dealing with this kind of situation. The bird seemed to extend the message leg toward him.

"Okay," Henry said, "alright. I get it. It's for me." He clicked on the flashlight and balanced it on the counter while he took the scrap of paper from the bird and unfolded it.

I am here, the note said, where are you?

Henry leaned against the counter, stunned. The bird turned around three times, then settled itself on the for-mica, tucked its head beneath its wing and went to sleep.

. . .

"Hey dude," Charlotte said, when her friend opened the front door. She held out a brown paper bag. "They had power at the LC," she said. "I brought wine."

"Great," Leah said hurriedly, her eyes a little wild. "Come in, come in." She grabbed Charlotte's sleeve and pulled her into the house.

"What's wrong?"

"Harold," Leah said, already turning away to race back up the stairs.

"What about him," Charlotte asked, following. She started to unwind her scarf, but got tangled up between it and the bottle of wine. She stopped, put the bottle down, left the scarf on and took the stairs two at a time after Leah. "It's warm in here," she said at the top of the stairs.

"I know," Leah wailed. "It's all my fault."

Charlotte caught up to her in the candlelit bedroom. "It's not a bad thing," she said.

"Yes, it is," Leah said. She leaned against the window sash, but it was stuck and wouldn't budge. "I forgot to open the goddamn window for Harold."

"Oh," Charlotte said. "Oh dear."

"Exactly," Leah grunted, still pushing at the window. "It's way past time for him to come home. Totally dark out now."

"What would he do if he got here and couldn't get in?" Charlotte asked. She stepped to the window and gave Leah a light push. "Let me try, Leah."

Leah stepped aside and wiped her hands over her face. "I don't know. What would he do? I don't know the answer to that."

Had Harold had tried to come home and found the window closed? Would he just go somewhere to wait, try again later? Maybe he was up in the eaves. With a mighty heave, Charlotte popped the window open. The wind rushed in, fluttering the red silk on Sandy's cage. Leah poked her head out into the freezing night. She twisted her neck to look up to the rooftop.

"Harold!" she called. She wasn't even sure if he knew his name, wasn't sure if birds could even hear, but she called for him again, just in case.

"Oh, sweetie," Charlotte said, her hand on Leah's back. Leah sighed, her hands on the windowsill, head still stuck out. The wind brought tears to her eyes. She closed them, and felt the water drip down onto her cheeks. She drew her head inside again.

"Now what?" Charlotte said.

"We wait," Leah said. "And we leave the window open." She grabbed two sweaters from the closet and handed one to Charlotte.

. . .

Henry closed the front door and wandered through the house with the flashlight, clutching the scrap of paper. What could it mean? Could it be for him? If not, why was the bird just hanging around in front of his house? Why had it flown inside without hesitation, gone to sleep, just like that, on his kitchen counter, for chrissakes? It didn't make sense that it could be for someone else. But at the same time it didn't make sense that it was for him. He was loath to rustle around in the kitchen for fear of waking the bird. He thought about playing his guitar, but that might disturb the creature too. Finally, he went upstairs and, resting the flashlight on the dresser, wrestled the clean sheets onto the bed. He put his socks and underwear in the drawer James had cleared out for him, and remembering his laundry in the basement, went down to see to it, the flashlight's aura bobbing in front of him, a spotlight he tried like hell to catch. Dry clothes to the dryer top, wet clothes into the drum, to wait for the power to come back on, then up the stairs with an armload of clean shirts and jeans, and then up the stairs again to put them away.

Just thinking about the note made his heart hammer in four-four time. Could it be from Tina? But then, what kind of sense did that make? She knew where he was, and he was pretty sure she didn't care. Come to that, he knew where she was, too. Big deal. It was done between them, for once and for all. And thinking about it now, he knew that was a good thing. They'd done little more than scrap the whole five years they spent together. In the beginning, that had been exciting. They'd have rousing arguments about—Christ; Henry didn't even know what they'd fought about back then, back before they had anything to fight about. Back before any of it mattered. Regardless they'd have astonishing, clattering fights then just as abruptly they'd fall into bed and have astonishing, clattering sex. The fights grew more intense, the sex, somehow, fell away. Till finally, all they were having were fights. And then, just before the very end, even the fighting had become simply commonplace. They fought wearily, about money, about Henry's supposed infidelity, about where they should live, about what they should have for supper. Once the passion went out of their fights, Henry had known it was over. It was just lying there waiting to die. And finally, one night, Tina put a bullet in its head and killed it. And in the end, Henry thought, it was a mercy killing. And now he was just waiting to get over it.

So it wasn't Tina then. And Johnny Parker knew damn well where to find him. And really, who else did he traffic with these days? It obviously wasn't that best-forgotten girl of last night. Maybe it was actually meant for James.

James was genuinely away, though not missing. He'd gone to England, on tour, and Emily had gone with him. Most everyone knew that, though, Henry thought, Christ, it was even written up in the newspaper. Big deal and all that. Good for James, and good for Henry. He had this place for another month if he wanted it, and he did.

Henry wondered if the bird would be hungry when it woke up. He wondered how long pigeons usually slept. He went down to the kitchen, and there the bird sat, placid, but most definitely awake. In fact, he thought, it looked a little hungry. He looked through the cupboard for something to give it, found a box of crackers, crumbled one up and mixed it with a bit of water. He put the paste on a saucer and placed it before the bird. "Bon apetit," he said, and the bird began to peck desultorily at the paste.

. . .

Nathan paced. Night was coming on. He hoped the bird had made it home, he hoped his message had been received. He could barely wait for morning, for another paper animal with a fortune cookie message.

. . .

Leah waited for Harold to come home. She had never waited so hard for anything.

. . .

Johnny Parker thought about going out. Maybe in a bit, he thought, and poured himself another drink.

. . .

Charlotte shivered in her sweater in Leah's living room and poured another glass of wine.

. . .

Henry looked out the window.

. . .

Leah looked out the window.

. . .

In front of the library, Nathan paced.

. . .

The phone rang, startling the bird. Henry picked it up. "Yeah," he said.

"Hey," said Johnny Parker.

"Oh, hey."

"What's going on?" said Johnny Parker.

"Right now?" Henry said. "Right now I'm staring at a pigeon on my kitchen counter."

"Dude. Seriously? The birds are taking over the neighbourhood, right?"

"Naw," said Henry. "Weird though. I come home, and there's this bird sitting in the road. It's got something on its leg. I'm a little bird shy these days, so I keep an eye on it while I'm getting in the house, and it flies in after me. Won't leave. Offers me its leg, for chrissakes, so I take this note off and it says, 'I'm here, where are you?' Whaddya think?"

"Who's it from?" Johnny Parker asked. He let out a stream of smoke against the receiver.

"No idea," Henry said. "No fucking clue."

"It's probably not even for you."

"Yeah, I thought of that," Henry said, "but—" he stopped. He hadn't told Johnny Parker about the voices he'd heard lately, the messages that seemed to be all around him.

"What," Johnny Parker said.

"Nothing," Henry said. "You're probably right. It probably isn't even for me. What do you think I should do with it?"

"Put it outside," Johnny Parker said. "Get shut of it."

"Yeah," Henry said, but he was reluctant. "Yeah, okay. I gotta go, I'll talk to you later."

"Wait, man, you coming out tonight?"

"Yeah, I don't think so," Henry said. "I think I'm done for the day. Gonna do some work."

On the counter, the bird finished the cracker paste. Henry pointed the flashlight at it, framing it perfectly in a circle of pale yellow light. It looked up from the saucer and watched Henry with one eye.

"Now what, birdie," Henry said. "What do you want now?" The bird cocked its head and looked at him some more. "You stay here," he told it. "I'll be right back."

He returned moments later with his guitar. He pulled out one of the kitchen chairs and had a seat. He tuned the instrument and strummed it meditatively a few times. "What do you want to hear?" he asked the pigeon. He hadn't had an audience in so long. This audience seemed as good a place to start again as any. "No requests?" he strummed some more. He played the song he always liked to start with;

its simple chords and sad words always gave him a strange kind of hope. And it seemed to fit the day, somehow, so he began: A then G, then each again, and into the Lightfoot lyrics he'd sung a thousand times before.

The bird tucked its head under its wing again and sighed.

. . .

Leah heard the song, but she didn't know where it was coming from. Maybe she was going mad. No bird, no ghost, that song coming from nowhere—it wasn't adding up to anything good. Maybe this was what cabin fever felt like. Maybe she'd driven herself mad, at last, with the staying inside, and the worrying.

Full darkness had swept across the street by now. What light there was from the moon bounced off the snow and reflected off the neighbours windows across the street. Leah thought it should look like a peaceful scene. But to her, it looked menacing, malevolent.

She looked at Charlotte, who was curled in chair, a flashlight she'd found in the kitchen cupboard tucked in beside her, hands pulled into her sleeves, reading.

"Do you think I'm going mad?" Leah asked.

"Hmmm?" Charlotte replied, barely looking up.

"Charlotte!" Leah said sharply. "Pay attention!"

"Sorry," Charlotte said, looking up. "This book is fascinating." She put the green hardcover down on the floor, held the flashlight under her chin so it made pools of light and darkness on her face. "It's very scary," she said, in her best Transylvanian accent.

Leah rolled her eyes in the darkness and waited while Charlotte chuckled at herself.

"Ah, that's funny," Charlotte said, then straightened up some, tucking the flashlight beneath her arm once more. "Sorry, honey, you had a question."

"I feel dumb asking now," Leah said. She took a deep breath. "Do you think I'm going mad?"

"Huh," said Charlotte. "Good question. Let's examine the evidence. You haven't left the house in a week, almost two, actually. You cook amazing meals all day, but you won't eat more than a bite. You hate and fear birds, yet you have two of them living in your bedroom because—and really, here's the punch line—you're using them to send messages to the ghost of your dead brother. What do you think?"

"On the face of it, sure," said Leah. "That all sounds like stuff you'd do if you were going mad." She rubbed her eyes. "God, I wish the lights would come back on. This would all be much easier if we weren't in the dark like this."

The wind pushed up against the windows, whining against the glass. The furnace had been off long enough that the cold was becoming its own creature, with sharp edges and an abrasive personality. It pressed against Leah's skin, leaving her hands and face feeling stripped and dry. Her feet, even in their two pairs of socks, were so cold they hurt. She wrapped her arms around her self and bent her head down to her chest, trying to get warm. Her breath was hot and humid, but fleeting. She could breathe into the room all she wanted, but the result was the same. Her breath barely lingered. Soon as she'd breathe in again, what she had pushed out into the room, her hot, alive contribution, would just become another molecule of frigid air. She sighed, producing more eventual frigid air.

"I don't think I'm going mad," she said at last. "I think I'm just really, really sad. And I wish I knew what else to do.

I wish I knew if it was working." She leaned her cheek on her knees and closed her eyes. Her black hair fell across her face like a curtain.

"This book says it should," Charlotte said, nudging it with her foot. "I mean, you've certainly nailed the indirect contact thing, anyhow. I still don't get it, though. I mean, I know what the book says and all. I'm just not sure I buy it. Don't you think this whole thing would be a lot easier if you'd just go down there and try to talk to him in person?"

Leah barely lifted her face from her knees. Her eyes stayed closed. "It doesn't work like that."

"Yeah, but why?"

"You read the book. Peter Pietropaulo says it in no uncertain terms. They don't like direct contact."

"Well, fine, then. Go down there and recite poetry to Nathan till he gets it."

Leah shook her head. "You just don't get it."

"You're right about that one," Charlotte said. She sipped her wine and looked at Leah over the rim of her cup. "You definitely have that one right."

"Look, I'm sorry," Leah said quickly. She didn't mean to be difficult, and she didn't want to anger Charlotte. The truth was, the book's information was in some ways convenient. The truth was she felt too guilty. It wasn't enough that she'd dropped out of sight those last six months of Nathan's life, but now she'd told him to get lost, and he had. It was taking forever to get him back to safety—which was not with her, she was more and more sure of that every day— and now one of the frigging birds was gone. Without Harold, Sandy would probably be useless and the whole thing was an unbelievable mess. She'd been no good to her brother while he was dying, and she was even less useful to him in his afterlife. It was too much to bear, really it was.

"I'm sorry," she said again. "I just feel on edge. It's Harold, the power-out, it's so freaking cold in here; it's everything. I can't go down to the library and talk to him, I just can't. I wish I could explain it to you, but I only half-understand it myself."

Charlotte pursed her lips to one side. "I'm just trying to help, Leah," she said.

"I know it. I know you are." She thought for a moment. "Hey, you know what? Maybe drop by the library some time and just let me know. Let me know what it's like there. If anything seems strange. If you think he's there, maybe."

Charlotte nodded. "I can do that for you." She thought of her regular visits to the library lawn to meet up with the hip-hop kid, the money and cigarettes that disappeared into his dirty parka, the neat parade of origami animals lined up behind the bushes against the library wall. Was it helping or not? If the pigeons had been returning home all this time with the origami still attached, Leah would be crushed. But she would have also had to find another way to get her message to him. Or maybe she would have let it go, let Nathan go. And maybe that would have been for the best.

"I can do that for you," she repeated, "if you think it will help." Charlotte wasn't sure she even believed in ghosts, herself. Maybe Leah could see Nathan. Maybe he was genuinely lost now. Or maybe something else was going on.

"It will," Leah said. "I really think it will."

"Well, you know more about it than me," Charlotte sighed, and Leah didn't bother to correct her.

"I'm going to check for Harold," she said, and stood up. She took a candle and climbed the stairs.

"Well?" Charlotte called after a few minutes had passed.

"No sign," Leah called back.

"Come on down then, wouldja," Charlotte said. "He'll come when he comes."

Leah came down the stairs, her face glum.

"Have you ever thought," Charlotte began, then halted.

"What?" Leah said.

"You're not going to like it," Charlotte cautioned.

"I can't remember the last time I heard something I liked. It's okay."

"Well, alright," said Charlotte. "Have you ever thought that maybe you should get Psychic Sue over here, see what she's saying?"

Leah laughed. "Um, it's because of Psychic Sue that I think heaven is a big meatball party."

"No," said Charlotte, "you think heaven is a big meatball party because you love Italian food. Seriously. Maybe Psychic Sue could tell you where Nathan is. I mean, isn't she the one who told you where he was the first time?"

"She was," Leah said. "She sure was. And it was kind of a shock." She thought about the last time she'd seen Sue. It hadn't gone well. She pushed it out of her mind. "I don't want to talk to Sue," she said firmly. "Maybe this whole thing is ridiculous. Maybe Peter Pietropaulo is wrong, though god I hope he's right. Or maybe it's all in my imagination. I mean, what is Nathan doing with me, anyhow? Shouldn't he be with Rebecca? Maybe he's with her now." She nodded her head slowly. "That's probably it. It's where he should have been in the first place, and she'll probably be a whole lot nicer to him than I've been."

"But what about the book?" Charlotte said. "How can you say it's ridiculous? You've put so much into it. I mean, the birds, for crying out loud."

"I know," Leah said. She rubbed the back of her hand across her eyes. "I'm just tired of it, you know? Maybe you were right in the first place. Ghosts are supposed to have access to things. Nathan should know his story; he shouldn't need me to tell it to him. And now Harold, and that just makes things so much worse somehow, you know?"

"Well, so what are you going to do?"

Leah shrugged. She started to answer, but she stopped, stiffened, waited, listened.

"What is it?" whispered Charlotte. "Is it Harold coming back?"

Leah held up her hands. "Listen," she barely whispered. "He's playing it again."

The strains of the guitar sidled in through the wall between the houses. Such a familiar melody. And then the voice, rising to meet the chords. The words were ones that had always made Leah cry, about ghosts and wishing wells, and the necessity of mind-reading.

Leah let her head drop into her hands. She cupped her forehead in her fingertips and just listened. She almost sang along, but she didn't want to lose the thread of the song. Nathan, she thought. I am here, where are you?

. . .

Warmed up now, and finally ready to work, Henry played the guitar for all it was worth. He played whatever came to mind. New songs he was still working on, old songs he'd written in school, cover songs, songs he'd sung when he was a child, songs he'd hated in the '80s but couldn't get enough of now. It was like his fingers were their own creature with their own agenda. His back ached from hunching around the guitar, but he couldn't stop playing. He'd slow down for a few minutes, but then his hands would catch their breath and they'd be off again. He laughed between verses. He hadn't felt like this in so long, or maybe he hadn't felt like this ever. The pigeon woke up and flew all around the room, in graceful dips and swoops, never once threatening Henry even a little, and Henry ducked and laughed, laughed and ducked. How incredible to be here, to be playing. I am here, he thought. And then he called it out to the bird: "I am here!"

. . .

Johnny Parker was in Hell, one of his favourite places to be. The beer was cold, the girls were hot and the music was loud. Always. That was the thing about Hell, it never changed. He loved it for that. He was starving he realised, as he drank his first beer of the night. He hadn't eaten much that day besides a bag of oatmeal raisin cookies, and Henry had had half of those. Henry. There was no accounting for that guy. Sure, he was a little messed up these days, what with Tina giving him the boot and all, but he was better off for it, he'd see that eventually, Johnny Parker was sure of it. Not that he'd shied away from telling Henry that soon as he got the call that Henry was out on his ass. But Henry hadn't been ready to hear that yet. And what little of it he did hear, Johnny Parker was sure, Henry'd chalked up to loyalty. He knew it, because he'd done the same thing himself every time Henry'd told him that he was well out of one situation or another. It took a while to believe it, that was all. But Johnny Parker was confident that some day soon, Henry would be ready. Jesus Christ, he thought, Tina was stepping out on him, and giving him a hard time about being faithful. That was just fucked, Johnny thought, taking another long swallow of beer. Now, wait a minute, food. He needed to get a good base coat down to cushion the prodigious amounts of alcohol he was planning to pour into his gut over the next few hours.

"Pizza ready yet?" he asked the bartender, who was a giant dude with greyish-blond dreadlocks.

"'Nother ten minutes," the bartender said.

"I'll have another drink till then," Johnny Parker said, and as he took a final swallow of beer, another frosty one appeared before him. Hell. It was a great place.

. . .

"Well I'd say the soufflé was a big success," Charlotte said, clearing away their dishes. Leah nodded.

"Yeah, not bad," she said, her voice small and dull. "I guess."

"And the cookies," Charlotte said brightly, trying to fill the space her friend used to fill, "so good! Hey, can I take some with me?"

"Sure," Leah said. She smiled a half-smile as Charlotte crammed a handful of cookies in her pocket.

"I wish you'd come with me, Leah."

Leah nodded. "Maybe another time. I'd better wait for Harold to come home."

Charlotte shook her head. "Okay," she said, "but I'll be at Hell if you change your mind, okay?" She put her coat on, wrapped her skinny scarf around her skinny neck and said, "I'll call you tomorrow. Don't stay up all night fretting about the bird. He's a homing pigeon, he'll come home, in his own time, okay?"

"Okay," Leah said. "Oh!" she said and jumped as if she'd been prodded. The lights had come back on.

"That's better," Charlotte said.

"Much." Leah smiled and closed the door behind Charlotte.

When the house was empty again, when she was alone, she sat on the steps and pressed her head to the wall. There was music there, still, music coming from the house next door. She closed her eyes and waited.

. . .

It was early yet. It'd be a while before the band was ready to hit the stage. Johnny Parker swung around on his barstool to see if he could see anyone he knew. Not yet. There was a smattering of NSCADets from the art school gathered at one table.

God knew what kind of ruckus they were planning. Like everyone else in town, Johnny had heard the beautiful rumours of naked parties at the Nova Scotia College of Art and Design. He'd never been to one, but he wanted to believe. This group was made up of guys and girls and a few kids in between. There were pixie cuts and dreadlocks, those androgynous hairstyles of the middle class art school crowd. The predominant fashion statement was patchwork, that and dresses over pants, on both guys and girls. Johnny Parker watched them with a mixture of admiration and impatience. They were certainly disconnected from the real world, though that was no reason to disdain them. Hell, Johnny Parker did what he could on a daily basis to lose his connection with the real world. And more than that he made a living playing guitar in a bar band. It could not be said of Johnny Parker that he lived in the real world. No way, not for an instant. And if you asked his father, he never had. But there was something too willfully playful about the NSCADets, that's what it was that disturbed Johnny Parker. Live and let live and all that, but these kids worked hard at being weird, or tragic, or sexually liberated or all three, and honestly, Johnny Parker found the whole thing a bit confusing. Then again, he reflected, it wasn't really for him, their show. At thirty years old, he was ancient to them, and meaningless, made more so by his status as part of a mostly-covers band. They were all about pushing the boundaries, and Johnny was all about selling beer.

And drinking it, for that matter. He raised his bottle to the art school kids, but if they noticed him doing so, they didn't respond. He could smell the pizza now. His stomach called out to it. He swung off the stool and went to check in with Sal.

Johnny leaned on the sill of the pizza bar. "Hey Sally," he said.

"Hey," said Sal. He was a flush-faced kid, maybe twenty-four. He wore an oversized paper-boy cap and his floppy hair pushed out from under it.

"What's cooking?" Johnny Parker said, pulling a smoke out of his pocket and lighting it up.

"I am," Sal said, hustling around the tiny kitchen. "Gimme a drag."

Johnny held the cigarette out. The kid stopped his hustling long enough to take a deep drag off the cigarette. He held the smoke inside for a couple of beats, then tilted his head to the ceiling and let it out in a slow, controlled stream.

"Whaddya want?" Sal said, once he was quit of smoke.

"Whaddya got?" Johnny Parker asked.

"Got pepperoni ready, veggie deluxe in the oven, be

about five, six minutes for that one, working on mushroom double cheese right now. Be fifteen minutes for that one."

"I'm not picky, dude," Johnny Parker said, reaching for his wallet. "Give us a slice of the pepperoni."

"Coming up," Sal shouted. He grabbed his pizza cutter from the magnetized board on the wall and whizzed it across the pizza. He turned the pie expertly with just his fingertips and made another incision. Another turn, another incision. Johnny Parker smoked and watched. Finally, Sal lifted a slice out, put it, dripping and giant, on a paper plate and handed it to Johnny, who gave him a couple of loonies in return.

"Thanks," Johnny Parker said. He handed over the rest of the cigarette. "Want this?"

Sal took it, stuck it in his mouth. "Anytime," he said and then he was back to hustling around the kitchen, cigarette dangling.

Johnny Parker turned away from the kitchen already mid-bite. Fucker was hot, and starting to stick to the roof of his mouth, but he was too far in to back out, and besides, there was a beautiful girl standing four feet away, staring at him.

Johnny chewed and fought the urge to spit the burning mouthful back onto the plate, and swallowed in a blazing gulp. He held the slice up to the girl and said, "Pizza?"

She laughed at him, her cap of brown curls bobbing. She looked like a fucking shampoo commercial, he thought, unbelievable. He moved toward her.

"Want a bite?" he asked.

"What kind?" she asked looking at it, and at him, with appraisal in her eye.

"Pepperoni," he said, "no one makes it better than Sally there." He shot his thumb over his shoulder in Sal's direction.

"Sure," the girl said, "I'll have a bite of that."

"I'm Johnny Parker," he said, handing over the pizza.

"Okay," the girl said, taking it from him and lowering her mouth to it. She looked up at him from under her bangs. "Thanks."

She took a bite; chewed it mouth slightly open.

"Hi's ho'" she said, steam pouring out of her mouth.

"Yeah," said Johnny Parker, "careful there it's really hot. Just came out of the oven. Kinda burns your taste buds off. I don't know why I don't blow on it, or wait awhile you know? Happens to me every time."

She looked at him politely, mouth still open, steam still pouring. She waved her hand in front of her mouth. He heard himself rattling on like his grandmother, who was a world class rattler who could talk for twenty minutes about what was on sale down the IGA. He wished he could shut up, but she was obviously in distress, and there was nothing he could think to do short of holding out his hand and inviting her to spit the pizza in it, and that was making him nervous, and damn it, Johnny Parker was not used to being nervous, and it turned out that when he was, all he could do was rattle like an old woman. So rattle he did.

"I play guitar," he said, mortifyingly. "I'm a musician."

She turned away from him, her body shook once and then she straightened up, mouth still agape. She reached for his beer, took a swig without asking. Not that Johnny Parker would have minded, just—well, she didn't seem to give a damn about anything, and here he was behaving like a twelve-year-old. A twelve-year-old grandmother. Jesus Christ.

She wiped her mouth with the back of her hand, smoothed down her hair with the palm of the other. "Huh," she said. "That so?" She reached for his beer again, took another deep draught of it. "That's better," she said. She gave her head a little shake, and those curls bounced again, mesmerising Johnny Parker. She looked at him pityingly, and finally said, "So, are you going to buy me a drink, or what?"

"A drink?" he said, as if he'd never heard of such a thing. "A drink, yes, of course, of course, I am. What, uh, what do you drink?"

"Tonight," she said, "I'm drinking JD."

"Coming up," Johnny Parker answered. He ordered the drink at the bar, looked back over his shoulder to make sure she was still there. She raised her eyebrows at him and he looked away fast. What a tool he was. How many girls, how many dozens, maybe hundreds of girls, and now all of a sudden it's the junior prom all over again? Jesus. He didn't even know her name. He got her drink and ordered another beer for himself. He turned to go back to her and she was right beside him.

"Oh," he said, "there you are." He handed her the Jack Daniels. "Um, there you are."

"Thanks," she said, taking it and knocking half of it back in one shot.

"Hey, I didn't catch your name."

"I didn't tell you my name," she said.

"That's true," Johnny Parker said. It was starting to grate on him how in a flap he was and how much she was enjoying and encouraging it.

"So, how about you tell me your name now," he said, gesturing to her drink with his beer hand.

"I will," she said, "but not because you bought me a drink. I'll tell you because I feel like it, and because you're kind of cute when you're flustered." She laughed a little, and put her hand in front of her mouth. It was clearly an act, but

Johnny Parker was willing to fall a little harder for it.

"Okay," he said. "Thanks, uh, thanks."

She smiled at him and held out her hand. "I'm Charlotte," she said, "and I'm charmed to meet you."

. . .

Leah woke up shivering and stiff. She'd fallen asleep on the steps, head pressed to the wall, and she awoke the same way. The music had stopped. The house was quiet. She shivered again, remembered the open window, the missing bird. She ran up the stairs, sure she'd see Harold pressed against the bars of the cage, trying to get in to be with Sandy.

But upstairs, there was still only one bird. Sandy sat unhappily in the cage, her seed dish empty, her partner missing, the room frigid and windy. Leah felt a wave of sympathy for the bird before her and a stab of worry for the one that hadn't come home. She poured some seed out into Sandy's bowl, filled her water bottle, and pulled the silk over the cage. She left the window open wide enough for Harold to squeeze through if—when—he came home. Then she took off her clothes and hurried into bed, pulling the duvet up to her chin and bringing her knees up to her chest. She waited for sleep as the wind that snuck through the window mussed her hair.

. . .

At the library, Nathan paced the paths up and down, up and down. Would the message get through? What would tomorrow's pigeon post bring?

. . .

Henry laid his guitar down to rest. The bird slept soundly on the kitchen counter, not stirring even when Henry finally put the groceries away. That done, his borrowed little house in order, he mounted the steps for his first well-earned sleep in weeks. God, the pleasure of sliding into a bed made with clean sheets, he thought. How could anything this simple feel so goddamn good? And if this was all it took, why hadn't he done the wash weeks ago? Didn't matter, it was done now. Henry closed his eyes and drifted off, a half smile on his face. Downstairs, the bird whistled in its sleep.

. . .

Charlotte and Johnny Parker circled each other like boxers in a ring. The band came on and played and was loud, but that didn't stop their conversation, that didn't change the way they looked at each other, that didn't solve Charlotte's desire to put her lips on Johnny's or Johnny's need to run his hand through Charlotte's curls.

"This is stupid," she said finally. "Why don't you just come home with me?"

Johnny Parker was on his feet in a heartbeat. He didn't even finish his beer.

They were barely in her door before he had her clothes off. He backed her towards the bed, as if they were two tango dancers. She worked at his belt buckle, peeled his jacket off, pulled at his shirt.

"I love you," he said, just before she fell backwards onto the mattress.

"Don't be ridiculous," she said, as he fell down after her.

. . .

Leah awoke with a feeling of dread. What was that about? Oh yeah. No bird. She opened both eyes, looked hopefully around the room. Still no Harold. It was freezing inside; the wind had calmed but wasn't quite gone. This had to end sometime. She couldn't keep the window open forever.

. . .

Henry awoke to find the bird sitting on his bedside table. It was the flapping of the wings that woke him.

"What's up pally?" he said. "Wanna go home?"

But the bird just looked at him and hopped off the table to the floor. It hopped to the hall then took flight, back downstairs to wait for Henry to get out of bed.

Henry did just that. He followed the bird downstairs, prepared another saucer of cracker mash.

"But that's it, little guy," he said, liking the sound of his voice, parental. "You've gotta get home, wherever that is." Next door, he wondered, thinking of he bird he'd watched wriggle in the upstairs window. He'd knock later, see if they were missing a bird next door, he thought. He put the saucer on the counter and the bird hopped over to it and began to peck. Henry watched proudly for a moment, then turned and began to fix himself some coffee. He pulled James and Emily's cafetiere from beneath the counter and filled the top with espresso. He ran water into it and put it to boil on the stove. He put bread in the toaster and fried an egg. He sliced a tomato and laid the slices on the egg in the frying pan. When the toast popped, he transferred the egg and tomato to the bread; spread some dijon mustard on one slice, added a leaf of lettuce and sat down at the table to eat. It was the first time he'd done that since coming to stay at James and Emily's, maybe even since well before that. He felt like a grown-up and that felt good. It was going to be a good day. The guitar leaned against the wall, ready when he was.

. . .

Johnny Parker woke up and nuzzled Charlotte's hair. "I'm sleeping," she said in a raspy morning voice. "Can't you see that?"

"I love you," he said.

"Don't be ridiculous," she said.

He kissed her shoulder and rolled away from her, got out of the bed. He reached for his tighty whities, pulled them on and padded to the bathroom. From there, he went to the kitchen, where he stood in front of the open fridge, scratching his belly. It wasn't promising.

Back in the bedroom, he got dressed as quietly as he could, but he was six-foot-four and not used to tiptoeing around.

Charlotte opened one eye.

"Sorry," he said.

"You leaving?" she said.

"Not exactly," he said. "Kind of."

"Whatever," she said and rolled over and began to snore gently.

Johnny Parker let himself out. Windsor Street was busy. What had been new snow the night before was now slush, and it splashed out of the road onto the sidewalk as the early morning traffic flew by. He waited for a break then dodged across the street to the corner store. There was a promising smell in the air, like rain instead of snow. It was the end of March after all, it couldn't last forever. He smiled and thought of Charlotte lying there in her bed, beautiful under blankets. Promising indeed. He didn't know what the hell was happening to him, but goddamn, he wasn't going to fight it. He bought eggs and bread and coffee and jam, and the Globe and Mail. He hoped she didn't have to work. He had no idea what she did for a living. He couldn't wait to ask her. He took the plastic bag of groceries, and whistling loudly, dashed back across the street to her apartment.

. . .

Leah was bereft. Harold was still MIA, and Sandy was inconsolable. She worried that if she sent Sandy out to deliver the message to Nathan, then both birds would be missing, because what if Sandy couldn't find her way back? If Harold was gone, was the cage still home to her? Leah didn't think she could take that chance. She hated to think of missing a day with Nathan, but it was only a day. Surely Harold would come back any minute, any hour, and then it would be solved. The message would just be a little late. She resolved to wait. The wind still clattered in the room. She pulled up the duvet over her ears and drifted back to uneasy sleep.

. . .

Henry knocked on the door next door. His fingers felt dry and shrivelled in the cold, windy morning. He waited, but no one came.

"I'll try again later," he said, to the closed door. Back inside, the bird still sat on the kitchen counter. Henry opened the window and waved toward it, but the bird wouldn't budge.

"Well," he sighed, "it's there if you want it." He put another log on the woodstove and pulled his turtleneck up around his ears.

. . .

Nathan and the hip-hop kid stood guard outside the library. That was how Nathan thought of it, though the hip-hop kid totally ignored him, didn't even know he was alive. The hip-hop kid asked people for change, but Nathan didn't. He just liked the feeling of having something to do. The bird was late, and he didn't know what that meant, but waiting for a response to his note felt like the hardest thing he'd ever had to do. So he stood with the hip-hop kid and it helped to pass the time.

. . .

"Go," Henry said, but the bird wouldn't go.

. . .

Come home, Leah silently commanded. But Harold simply wouldn't.

. . .

"You're incredible," Johnny Parker said, his hands caught in Charlotte's hair.

"You're not so bad yourself," Charlotte said, and she kissed him square on the lips.

. . .

Leah stood in the gathering gloom. In spring and summer, her study was flooded with light, but in winter it got dark so quickly. The lack of light made working in there all day difficult. The clutter wasn't helping. Leah was determined to change the things she could. She moved through the room, making piles of things that could go, things to keep, things to put in the basement. She stopped in front of the Hardy Boys bookcase, the guitar leaning palely up against it. She could not consign what was left of Nathan to the dank, cold basement. She just couldn't. She didn't want to go back, and she wouldn't go forward. She just churned in neutral.

. . .

A whole day had passed, and here came the night, and no bird. Nathan sat on the library steps and hugged his knees. He wondered if it was something he'd said. He laid his cheek on the platform his knees made and waited for the bird to come back.

. . .

Henry put another log in the woodstove, pulled his hand back from the crackling sparks. He nudged the bird toward the open window. "Go," he said. But the bird wouldn't go. Henry sighed. He'd have to leave the window open all night.

. . .

Leah began to know that waiting was futile. She stood before the case of Hardy Boys books and knew. He was just a stupid bird, and Leah didn't even like birds, but losing him was like losing Nathan all over again. She couldn't keep anything, anymore. She put her head down and cried.

. . .

The Ferris wheel kept spinning long after the music had stopped. Henry stood staring at it, absently winding up his various cords and cables and putting his pedals away in their bag. The lights on the Ferris wheel twinkled in the late afternoon; some distant, better city, always in motion.

It hadn't been the best gig he'd ever played, but neither had it been the worst. Without question, though, it was the only gig he'd ever played where half the audience was upside down or hurtling through the air and screaming their guts out. He could only imagine it made the music sound better to them.

The Place Holders were just what their name suggested. They played covers. They plugged holes. In lineups and in Henry's income. They'd do, till something better came along, both for the audience and for him.

He appreciated the opportunity to rock out with Johnny Parker. He was always glad to get a chance to hang toes off the edge of the stage and shred. Even if it did mean playing "Sweet Home Alabama" every night. He'd give it everything he had; play his guitar hard, behind his head while Johnny wrapped himself around the mic stand, as if they were rock stars.

Still, the amusement park scene? He could do without it. You played your heart out for people who didn't know a damn thing about music. For people who didn't care to hear anything they'd never heard before. You played outside in winter, for chrissakes, and you might as well run your fingers over a set of freshly bought steak knives as play an electric guitar outside in subzero temperatures. It wasn't taking him anywhere, these piddling little fairground winter carnival gigs. But it was two hundred bucks in his pocket, and he wished he didn't need it, but he did. He shook his head and turned away from the Ferris wheel, back towards his guitar case.

Parker had his instrument all packed up, the soft case slung on his back like a machine gun he wasn't using. He raked a hand through his damp blond hair, then blew out, and moved the bangs off his forehead with his breath.

"You going out tonight?" Johnny asked.

Henry snapped the clasps on his guitar case. "Nah. I don't think so, man. I've gotta get at these songs." He stood the case on its end, willing to be convinced.

"You sure?" Parker said. "Marko Marks is playing at The Awkward Stage. And then it's the open mic. It's going to be a massive show."

"I don't know," Henry said. He thought ruefully of the time he'd already spent that day on garbage, on nothing. The endless fairground sound check, as if it mattered at all in a place where the best you could do was to try to compete with the screams of giddy fairgoers. "I gotta stop fucking around some time."

"Fair enough," Parker said. He shifted, repositioned his guitar on his back. "Totally reasonable. But dude, this guy's a legend, man. And when are you ever going to see him again, especially in this town?" He punched Henry's hunched shoulder. Henry flinched. "Total respect if you can't do it. I can dig that, man. But man, it's gonna rock."

Henry bunched his shoulders a little further up toward his ears. The songs were not exactly going to write themselves. With every night that went by, Henry felt them moving further away, felt the juice bar moving inexorably closer. As if his life were a rope dotted with buoys, its possibilities and probabilities, climaxes and eventualities strung out along it and all he could do was pay it out a little at a time, or feel it zip through his hands as he sped further away from what he wanted. He knew he was dropping himself clues, markers for where these things lay in his life. But at some point, he would have to come back, navigate back through these waters and haul up the traps. See what lay beneath, what he'd left behind for himself. Still, though. Parker was right. Marko Marks. And he already had his guitar, it wouldn't kill him to play a few tunes at the open mic, either. That was like working, he reasoned.

"What the hell," he said at last. He lifted his guitar case. "Let's go."

"Good man," Johnny said, slapping Henry's back. "Atta boy."

The Awkward Stage was crowded, but Johnny and Henry shuffled and bumped their way to the bar. They parked their guitars beneath it, standing them up on their ends. "Beer," Johnny said to the woman behind the bar. "Make it two," Henry said. "Ten Penny," he clarified. She nodded and turned away.

"Busy," Parker said. Henry nodded. His stomach felt jumpy. Guilt, maybe. The beers came, and Henry took a long swallow off his. It was cool and hoppy. It hit the spot.

"Yeah, the place is full," he said. He turned to the bartender. "Has he already played?"

She nodded. "First set, yeah. It's his break. He'll play again, though."

Henry smiled and raised his beer bottle in salute. "Thanks." He turned and leaned his back against the bar again.

"Dude," Parker said. "I met a girl."

Henry stopped, his bottle raised halfway to his mouth. "Really," he said, drawing the word out. This was interesting. Johnny Parker met girls all the time—hell, it would be a remarkable night for him if he didn't meet a girl—but he never felt a need to report these meetings as if they were something. "What girl did you meet?"

"Her name's Charlotte," Johnny said. "She's awesome, man. Beautiful. Smart. Sexy."

"That's pretty much the holy trinity," Henry said.

"Don't I know it," said Johnny. He raked his hand through his hair. "I'm fucked."

Henry looked at his friend. It was true, Parker looked done in. Henry couldn't put his finger on it exactly, but there was something different in Johnny's face. Something open that had previously been closed.

"Good luck with that," Henry said, lifting his beer bottle in his friend's direction. "It sounds terminal."

"Yeah," Johnny said. "That's kind of what I'm afraid of. Oh hey," he gestured to the stage with his beer. "Check it out."

A band was assembling on the small stage in the far corner of the room. Drums, bass, guitar.

"Have you seen this guy before?" Johnny asked as a tall man with long black hair strapped on a cherry red electric guitar.

"No, never," said Henry.

"Man, he's going to blow your mind," Johnny said. And if he elaborated on that thought it was lost in the first blast of music, a blast that parted Henry's hair and rearranged his internal organs. He squinted at the stage for forty-five minutes and at the end of it, wondered if he should check his skin for blisters.

"Christ," he said, as the final chords died away.

"Yeah, I know," Parker said. "I'm going to tell that guy he rocks."

"I bet he knows," said Henry.

"Shut up, dude," said Johnny.

Henry hated the end of show gathering around the guitar god of the week. He couldn't stand feeling like a sycophant, even if—especially if—he genuinely admired someone's work. Instead, he drained his beer and went to get on the open mic list.

"Put me up first, wouldja?" he asked, "I gotta get home some time."

. . .

Leah tried to sleep. She had left the window open in the hopes that Harold would find his way home. And though she was tired, Sandy's restlessness led to her own. The bird cried and turned relentlessly in the cage. Leah pulled the duvet up around her ears, to try to stay warm and block out the plaintive sounds. "It's too much," she said aloud, her breath pooling in the cold darkness. "It's just too much. It has to stop. It has to stop some time." She wasn't sure who she was talking to, who she expected to call a halt to things. She thought about God who always seemed like yellow crayoning, a hand, some feet, the clouds. She wondered if God ate meatballs. More and more, heaven was starting to seem like a complex of condos in Florida. Retirement homes, populated by all kinds. And God, she imagined, was the superintendent. He must be busy fixing someone's faucet, Leah thought. Because still Sandy cried, and still Harold didn't come home.

. . .

Henry felt good. The crowd had thinned out some, but not much. The room's mood remained buoyant, and he felt like he was bobbing on its friendly sea. It was a little strange to have his electric on his knee instead of his acoustic, but whatever. The songs were what they were, no matter how he played them. They either worked or they didn't. He felt like he'd find out, one way or the other. He felt nervy. Like he was in love. But maybe he was just projecting how Johnny must be feeling. Johnny, who had left early after fielding a cell phone call. "Gotta go, my man," he'd said, and winked. "Gotta go," Henry had agreed.

Moments later, MJ had called Henry's name, and there he was on stage. There were a few familiar faces in the crowd. It didn't matter. The only thing that mattered was playing the songs. Henry cleared his throat into the mic. The noise level in the room increased a hair then subsided Henry shrugged.

"Here goes," he said into the mic. Nothing, he said, in his mind. He closed his eyes, found his place on the fretboard and was away.

He had no illusions that his songs would bring some kind of magical change upon the room. The Awkward Stage was a somewhat dingy bar, perennially well attended, so it didn't have to try too hard with décor or menu. You could get nachos or poutine, or chicken strips if you were feeling hungry. You could get draught beer or bottled, or mixed drinks. The bartenders smiled, but only as much as they had to. The stage was small but mighty. The best came to play here, but so did the worst. There were open mics most nights and you never knew what you were going to see. Most nights, you saw a lot of crap. But once in a while, someone took your breath away.

Henry was having a good night. The level of conversation in the room stayed steady, or maybe abated a little. It was hard to tell from where he was sitting. But it didn't get louder, and no one called for him to leave the stage. He'd seen that happen. Not often to someone like him, someone who knew how to be on stage, knew how to work a crowd, when to woo them with stories, with details about each song, when to simply shut up and play. Henry had a certain amount of confidence that he had every right to stand where he stood, his guitar sturdy on its leather strap. Usually, guys in his league were safe at The Awkward Stage, but not always. Henry had seen it go ugly, fast. But tonight was different. Tonight, Henry could do no wrong. He sang four songs, to healthy applause after each. By the end of his fourth song, there were whistles. Some tapped the tabletops with their beer bottles. Henry grinned, nodded at the audience, thanked them and, in his head, thanked Yahweh, Allah, the Universe, whoever was responsible. It had gone alright. It wasn't much, but it was something, and it had gone alright.

Afterward, he put his guitar back in its case for the second time that night. He folded up the hem of his t-shirt, used it to mop his brow. It was fucking hot. His t-shirt was damp already, and couldn't accommodate much more. But he mopped anyhow.

He felt a hand on his back. "That was great, man."

"Thanks," he said, twisting around to see who it was. A guy he didn't recognise. "Yeah, thanks a lot. It was fun."

"Looked like it," the guy said. His hair curled slightly, artfully, around the collar of his expensive-looking leather jacket. He sized Henry up with canny brown eyes. "Dave O'Dell," he said, sticking out his hand.

Henry took it, shook. "Henry Menard."

"Nice songs," Dave said. "They all yours?"

"Yeah," Henry said. "I've been writing a lot lately. Still working out some rough patches with them, but they're coming along.

"Have any more like that?" Dave asked.

"A few," Henry said. "A few more I'm still working on."

Dave nodded, reached into his pocket and smoothly pressed his card into Henry's hand as he shook it again. "You get them finished," he said, "you call me."

Henry nodded dumbly, closed his fingers around the business card. He managed to keep himself from holding it up in the dim bar and scrutinising it—at least until Dave O'Dell turned and walked away. Henry clutched the card in his hand as if it were the key to untold secret riches. He hustled to the urinal-cake-stinking bathroom and held the card up in the light. Dave O'Dell, it said, Independent Record Producer. And then a list of awards Dave O'Dell had won. Henry raised his eyebrows at himself in the mirror then slid the card into his pocket. One more beer, and then he'd go home. Tomorrow, he'd have his work cut out for him.

. . .

Leah slept fitfully, shivering even beneath her duvet. In

the morning, when she woke up, Sandy was dead. She was backed against the furthest corner of the cage, cold and stiff, her eyes dull instead of gleaming. The wave of revulsion Leah had first felt toward the birds returned, but she felt hot tears on her cheeks all the same. Sandy had cried all night with increasing fretfulness, finally stopping around four in the morning. Leah, grateful, had thought she'd merely exhausted herself. Herself exhausted, Leah had slept. But now this. Dead of a broken heart, Leah had no doubt. Could things get worse? First Nathan missing, then Harold, and now this. A dead bird because of her. Everything she touched turned to rust.

Leah took the red silk off the cage and laid it in a shoebox. She reached into the cage and pulled Sandy out. The bird was stiff and cold, its feathers more grey than brown now. She placed the bird gently in the shoebox, wrapped the red silk around the frigid body, and covered the whole thing with the lid. She wondered if there was something else she should do, and wished she'd loved the bird even a little.

. . .

Nathan was at the end of his rope. Two days now and no reply. Every time a bird circled over the library, he balled his hands into fists and held his breath. And every time the bird failed to land on the step in front of him, he let the breath out slowly and stood stock-still on the path in front of the library, trying to regain his equilibrium. It didn't make sense. Obviously, he'd offended someone with his note, but who? And why were they writing to him in the first place if they didn't want him to write back? It defied logic. And logic was Nathan's mother tongue.

The afternoons were proving long without an avian visit. Nathan wished he had the patience to read, but he felt he had to keep moving, and he didn't think he could read and walk at the same time. Besides, he could never seem to get anyone's attention in the library. Even if he had wanted to borrow a book, he doubted he would have been able to.

Maybe the bird was on its way. Maybe his correspondent was simply trying to find the right words. Nathan resolved to wait a little longer. He didn't know what else to do.

. . .

Johnny Parker was getting ready to take a shower. He whistled. He couldn't help it. He wasn't sure what he'd done to deserve what he had—whatever that was. He was pretty sure he was in love, as ridiculous as that sounded. He stood in Charlotte's bathroom and whistled, and scratched his bare chest. She was remarkable. But he had to be careful, he figured. He had his life carefully arranged for maximum pleasure. He went out when he wanted and came home when he wanted. And while he was out, he did what he wanted. If he and Henry wanted to smoke dope all day and eat cookies, there was no one to answer to. And he liked that, he really did. On the other hand, Charlotte. Shiny-haired, hilarious Charlotte.

Johnny Parker ran the hot water. He stepped out of his boxer shorts. He decided not to decide anything. He'd just go along, he thought, and see where he ended up. He got the water where he wanted it and stepped beneath the spray.

. . .

Leah straightened up the stack of origami paper on the kitchen counter. She wondered if she should make a little animal for Sandy, a little bird to keep her company in her cardboard box. She missed the daily routine. She missed Harold. And most of all, she missed Nathan.

She wasn't sure how she would dispose of Sandy's body. She pushed the shoebox to the back of the counter and left the kitchen. She didn't even bother to put on a pot of coffee.

. . .

Charlotte genuinely couldn't think of how she'd filled her time before that night in Hell. Her stupid job, she guessed. That thing took up a lot of time. But she'd called in sick once already, and she didn't think she could again. It had meant she'd had to stay in all day, in case anyone from the office saw her and busted her, but going out didn't appeal to her. Staying in with Johnny Parker did. It would have to end sometime, she supposed. Even if the relationship continued, which was highly unlikely, she had to admit, this honeymoon phase couldn't last forever. And anyhow, she had to go back to work. The lawyers needed their cases researched, and they were pretty much useless without her.

But she liked the way Johnny laughed, and the way he made everything seem possible. "It's positive, man," he'd say, when things were going well. And "man, that's a drag," when they weren't. He was straightforward and open and Charlotte liked that about him.

She wanted to tell Leah, and she didn't want to. It didn't seem fair, with all her friend was going through, to turn up so gleefully happy. Then again, perhaps Leah could use the distraction, Charlotte thought. She picked up the phone and dialed.

. . .

Henry woke up early, on top of the world. Dave O'Dell's name rang in his ears like the best line from the best song he'd ever heard. Correction: from the best song anyone had ever heard. A song he'd written. It was a short step from the open mic at The Awkward Stage to world domination, he could feel it. Dave O'Dell was the bridge.

Henry laid on his back and felt invincible. His cock was morning-hard and he felt like the most powerful man on earth. He was going to write. All day. And he was going to slay.

. . .

Charlotte kissed Johnny Parker goodbye for the second time that morning. Once didn't seem to be enough. She'd thought it was going to be, but then she'd gotten to the door and had to come back for more. Didn't seem to bother him any. He smiled broadly when he saw her coming, held his arms open to her, picked her up and swung her around. Her hair flew out, shiny. He loved her.

"Okay, put me down," she said, a little breathlessly. "I mean it, I have to go. Leah needs me."

"I need you," Johnny said, putting her down and pinching her ass.

"Oh, you've had me. That'll hold you." She winked at him and squirmed out of his arms.

"I don't know if it will," he called after her. "I'm already starting to fade. I'm fading fast. Don't be cruel."

She laughed, waved, blew a kiss and was out the door.

. . .

The house was freezing cold when Henry got up. He shivered in his shirtsleeves, and stoked up the fire again. He wondered if the bird was gone. In the kitchen, the saucer was empty. He put the coffee on to brew, and had a look around the house. No bird. It was a relief. He shut the kitchen window and waited for the coffee to make. Gonna be a good day, he thought.

. . .

Charlotte knocked and waited, knocked and waited. She entertained a brief hope that Leah might have actually gone outside, but soon she saw her through the door's window, coming heavily down the hall. She was carrying a shoebox. Oh boy, Charlotte thought. Here we go.

She took a deep breath and smiled gently at Leah when the door swung open.

"Thanks for coming," Leah said. She clutched the box dumbly. "I—stupid birds, you know?"

"Yeah," Charlotte said. She unwound her scarf and shut the door behind her. "I know, honey."

"Just," Leah said, "I think the ground might be soft enough to dig. I've been listening to it melt out back for two days."

"Don't worry," Charlotte said, "I'm sure it will be fine. Do you have any coffee?"

Leah's nose reddened, just at the tip.

"Oh no," said Charlotte, "No, don't do that. It's okay. Tea is fine, just fine."

"It's not that," Leah said, her voice already wet with crying.

"What then? The bird?"

Leah shook her head. "No, well, yes, a little, but no, not the bird. It's me, this house, Nathan," the words galloped out. "This whole thing is a joke. It was a bad idea to try it this way. He's gone and that's all there is to it, you know? I can't—birds, origami, messages—none of it changes anything. It's not—none of it matters, it doesn't matter. It's just, he's gone, and I can't find him, and no matter what I do, that doesn't change. He's just gone." She cried freely, the tears dripping off the end of her nose, plummeting from her cheeks to her sweater, dripping onto the worn softwood floor, settling in, becoming part of the house.

Charlotte put her arm around her sobbing friend.

"And it's so stupid, you know? I'm so weak. I'm so, I think I'm special, somehow, that what I feel is different, but it's not, you know? It's exactly the same."

Charlotte patted Leah's black hair, smoothed it down over her shoulders. "Sweetie, you're not making any sense."

Leah laughed damply against Charlotte's shoulder. "It's okay," she said, with a mouthful of tear-soaked hair, "it makes sense to me. I've been an idiot. I'm going to try to stop." She drew away from Charlotte, pushed the wet hair off her face, patted Charlotte's shoulder. "Sorry," she said.

"Don't apologise," Charlotte said. "It's what I'm here for." Charlotte picked up the shoebox and moved toward the back door. "I'll go bury this thing. Uh, Sandy."

"Thanks," Leah said. She could barely look at her friend. She leaned against the kitchen counter, in view of the backyard, but several feet from the door.

Outside, Charlotte placed the shoebox on the bench and began to dig with a spade she'd found against the shed. The ground was still mostly frozen and it took a while, but she was able to dig out a good-sized hole behind the lilac bush. Charlotte plunked the shoebox in the hole.

She stood in silence for a moment then looked back over her shoulder at Leah who stood at the kitchen window, her face a pale painting in the window's frame.

Finally Leah shrugged. Charlotte shrugged too, leaned the shovel back where she'd found it, rubbed her hands together briskly and came back inside.

"Should I say something, a few words?" Charlotte asked, the door clicking shut behind her.

"It was just a bird," Leah said. But a whirring flash of grey-brown in the backyard made her stop. She looked up and out the window again. "Harold," she said. "For chrissakes." Harold came to rest on the mound of snow-streaked dirt beside Sandy's grave.

"Jesus," said Charlotte, "are you sure?"

"Yeah, look at his leg." The message sheath was there, and it was empty. "Where have you been," she said sternly, face pressed against the glass. "Look what's happened now."

Charlotte opened the door, stepped out into the yard again.

Leah pulled the door shut, shivered.

Charlotte moved toward the makeshift gravesite. She shooed Harold off the mound, and shovelled it back into the hole, patting it down with the spade. Harold flitted about from branch to branch on the lilac bush, and when Charlotte was done, Harold flew toward it, alit there and looked steadily at Charlotte till she backed away and went inside.

Leah put the coffee on. There was always coffee after a

funeral. Coffee with real cream because who cared at that point? And sandwiches with lots of mayonnaise, cut in quarter triangles. She rummaged through the fridge. "No sandwiches," she said.

"What?" Charlotte said, running warm water over her hands.

"No sandwiches. Not much of a reception."

Charlotte looked at her blankly.

"For the funeral," Leah said. She looked at Charlotte looking at her. "I'm cracking up, aren't I?" she said.

"A little," said Charlotte. "A little, you are."

"Anyhow," Leah said. "We have coffee. No cream though. And we have goat cheese and crackers."

They took their mugs to the front room and drank the coffee in silence while the sounds of guitar music came from next door.

"I should go," Charlotte said finally. "I'm way behind at work now, thanks to Johnny Parker." She blushed a little just from saying his name.

"Whoa," Leah said. "Who the hell is Johnny Parker?"

"I don't know," Charlotte said, reddening further. "This guy I met."

"So that's where you've been," Leah said, smiling with her eyes. "I'm going to need details."

"I know," Charlotte said. She stood up and shrugged into her coat. "But for now I have to go to the office and pretend to be recovering from the 'flu."

"Good luck with that," Leah said.

"Mmm hmm," Charlotte said dreamily, winding her scarf around her neck. She put a hand on Leah's arm. "And for real, Leah, I am so sorry about the bird."

"I'll be okay," Leah said. "Go, you don't want to get fired."

. . .

Nathan waited. He couldn't believe a second day could go by with no birds, but then, if he thought back, and thinking back wasn't easy for him, but he could do it if he tried, if he really concentrated hard, if he thought back, the birds hadn't always come. There had been a number of days when he'd just been by himself, waiting. He didn't know what he was waiting for at the time, but now he knew. He was waiting for the birds. But now that the birds had stopped coming, he didn't know what he was waiting for next. But it was all he knew how to do, so he gathered his hands into loose fists at his sides to keep his arms from flapping the way they had when he was a child, and he took the library path, back and forth, back and forth.

. . .

Henry sat with the guitar on his knee and thought about Tina. He pictured her, and he pictured Rene, her picky old artist boyfriend, and he wondered how he felt. Truth was, he didn't feel much of anything. And that felt kind of good. Something was happening, he could feel it. He reached across his guitar and pushed record on his four-track, just in case. Then he went back to his instrument, and listened to what it was saying.

. . .

Charlotte tried to concentrate on her work, she really did, but every time she licked her lips, she thought about Johnny Parker. She spent half an hour emailing herself a list of things she liked about him. Then she spent another half an hour thinking about what to get him for his birthday. Then she spent half an hour simply staring into space. At the end of that, she got up, put on her coat and said to the office in general, "I don't feel well. I think I'd better go home."

She called Johnny Parker from the payphone on the corner, and he said, "Baby, I thought you'd never call. You come right on over." And she did.

. . .

For two whole days, Harold sat on the mound beneath the lilac tree and cried. He cried so plaintively Leah worried that he would die too, that the next time she looked out the window, it would be to see his dull grey bird carcass heaped on Sandy's grave. But near the end of the second day, he went quiet. She ran to the window to make sure he was alive. He looked at her once, took wing and flew away. She knew she'd never see him again.

. . .

It was three days now, and still no birds. Nathan couldn't believe it. He paced, he sat, he twisted his hands, he thought about Winston Churchill and still no birds. No birds, no notes, no Leah, no Rebecca, no anyone he knew. The closest thing he had to a friend these days was that hip-hop kid in the dirty parka, and even he didn't come around much anymore. Nathan sighed, drove his hands into his pockets. He supposed he'd have to think seriously about getting home soon. Rebecca would be worried, and though he liked the library, its charms were beginning to wear thin. Nathan was tired of being ignored, he wanted to go home, where people knew who he was, where they cared about him, where they missed him when he wasn't around. He curled up in the bushes and thought about how to get home, how to figure out where home was from here.

. . .

Leah filled another bag with clothes she didn't need. She hoped they'd send a big truck and a crew of able-bodied guys. She had so much she wanted to get rid of.

. . .

Henry raided James's closet for more good dress duds. He felt great in James's clothes, and in James's house, and he allowed himself to fantasise that James and Emily would never come home, and that he, Henry, could simply slide into this new, ready-made life. He loved going up and down the stairs, having a bathtub, doing laundry in the basement. He loved the solitude. He loved not fighting with anyone but himself, and then only if he really felt like it. He loved stretching out in the whole bed, getting up when it suited him, playing guitar if he wanted all day long. He realised he didn't miss Tina, not for herself. He was hurt that she'd cheated on him, mad that she couldn't even admit it, sorry for her that she'd had to turf him out rather than deal with herself. But he wasn't sorry for himself. Getting kicked out was the best thing that had happened to him in a long time. Since—well, since he'd hooked up with Tina in the first place. He whistled while he dressed, looked at the clock. Whoops, he was late. Oh well, Johnny Parker would expect that. And besides, he'd be all distracted by the new girlfriend. Henry had to admit there was a curiousity about her. He'd never heard Johnny Parker go on and on quite the way he was inclined to with this one. Charlotte was her name. He was keen to get a look at her. He took a last look in the mirror, raised an eyebrow at himself, then clattered down the steps, grabbed his coat and flew out the door.

. . .

Nathan sat up short. He suddenly remembered who he was waiting for. It wasn't Rebecca at all. It was Leah. He was done for. She was never on time. He might as well make himself comfortable. He curled back down beneath the bushes and tried to go to sleep. He'd long since given up trying to make any sense of the notes he'd been sent, but it comforted him to have them close. They were flattened out now and dirty from having been whipped about in the windstorm. But he'd managed to corral them all together again in the bushes. He let his eyes linger on each one in turn.

A long flight, only sorrow at the end.
A gathering storm, you kept time with your breath.
The bell in the night calls us and we come.
The tether slips, you slide, you soar.
After midnight, in the silence, intensive, the machines turned
    away discreetly, as if to grant you privacy at last.
A feeling of relief in the quiet room. The heat subsides.

CHARLOTTE AND JOHNNY PARKER WERE HOLDING HANDS.

"Good night?" he asked as they passed in front of the library, on their way home from drinks with Henry.

"Good night," she nodded. "I like your friend."

"Henry," he said. "Yeah he's a good cat. Guy's been through some hard times lately, for sure, but it seems like things are turning around for him."

"It's exciting about that producer," Charlotte said.

"Could be," Johnny said. "Could be very positive. As long as he keeps a steady hand on it now. So long as he doesn't freak-out."

Charlotte nodded. "Seems like it," she said.

. . .

Where the hell was Leah? Nathan groused to himself. He'd been waiting half the night, and it looked like he was going to have to wait the other half as well. As long as it didn't rain, he'd be okay. But still, he would rather be anywhere else. His patience with the library had finally worn thin. He grooved himself deeper into the dirt between the bushes and the wall and closed his eyes again.

. . .

Leah slept fitfully. In her dream it was that night, that terrible night outside the library. She was drunk, stinking drunk, and she could feel Nathan's eyes on her, but every time she turned around, he'd look away. He was driving her crazy. She was old enough; she didn't need a babysitter. And anyway what was he good for? He'd gone and left her. Oh, she was mad. She'd leaned on the wall at the library and tried to stop the spinning in her head, but every time she looked up, Nathan. It had been the same all goddamn day, and she was sick of it. There he was, with those big eyes, those big haunted eyes, and he would never look right at her. But he would be there, just standing there. Suffering, because of her. Finally, it was enough.

"Fuck off," she roared, her hands thrown up in front of her face. "Just get the fuck away from me! I can't stand it anymore. I don't want you here, so leave me alone."

And just like that, she felt him leave.

She had thought, when he still lived, that when he died, she would know it. Would feel him go, maybe even see him once before he left. But when that time came, she was oblivious. She'd been asleep, deeply so, and had been torn from unconsciousness by the bright light of her bedside lamp, and her mother's hand on her back. It's time. Time for what, she wondered, groggy and disoriented. And then she remembered. Ah. Time.

But in this dream, and on that night in front of the library, she had indeed felt him leave. A cold wind, a tearing sound, and then she was without him. Drunk, and thinking she was happy, she stumbled home. It wasn't till she got to her front door that the goosebumps started, the prickling horror.

And it was only the next morning that she really saw what she had done. She'd chalked up to her hangover her nervousness, her unease at the thought of being outside. Grimly, she'd shoved her feet into her boots and struggled the three blocks to the organic market for carrot juice and whole grain raisin bread. Some people craved fried potatoes and endless cups of black coffee after a night on the town, but Leah always hungered for virtue in the aftermath.

She was grubby and unbathed, intending only to grab her juice and bread and shuffle home again. But as soon as she pushed open the door, heard its little bells chime, she was met with Psychic Sue. Leah took a deep breath. Psychic Sue was exactly the wrong kind of intense for Leah's state of being. She insisted on having only deep conversations, and on making deep eye contact. Leah was feeling more surface. She wanted a shallow connection, the kind where you waved then looked away quickly.

Granted, Psychic Sue had been somewhat more tolerable since the reading she'd given Leah, but there were still parts of that whole thing that were beyond puzzling. Her brother had had no kids, wasn't even married. Perhaps he'd intended to propose to Rebecca, but he got sick before he had the chance, and was too responsible to ask her to tie herself down to a cancer patient once he was diagnosed. So Sue's predictions about her nephews seemed impossible to say the least. And then there was her own supposed Cheshire Cat grinning future husband. That in itself was an unbelievable crock.

Leah shook her head. It didn't have the desired effect of clearing her thoughts. If anything, the sudden movement clouded them. Psychic Sue was right there, and about to say hello, when the look on her face changed from happy to deeply disturbed.

"Hey Sue," Leah had said. "How's it going?" She steeled herself for the inevitable conversation about whatever healing techniques Sue was learning and experimenting with.

"Hey."

Leah raised her eyebrows and waited for more. It was impossible that she could get off so easily.

Sue's eyes kept darting to Leah's left shoulder. She looked increasingly distraught.

"What's up?" Leah persisted. It was nothing short of bizarre that Sue wouldn't engage her. Perhaps Leah still reeked of alcohol. That was very likely, she considered.

Sue took a step away from her, still glancing repeatedly at Leah's shoulder. "I have to go," Sue blurted at last.

"Okay," Leah said. She couldn't smell the vodka herself, but obviously, Sue could.

"I have to go to a consciousness raising class," Sue said. She abandoned her cart, pulling her knapsack out of it and pushing past Leah in a hurry.

Leah shrugged. She got her juice and bread and headed for home.

As she made her way, she thought about Psychic Sue's odd behaviour.

She used her cell phone to call Charlotte. "Weirdest thing," she said. "She was so twitchy and strange. She said she had to get to her consciousness raising class."

"A psychic needs to have her consciousness raised?"

"I know," Leah said, "it's like, wouldn't you be hoping to have it kind of, I don't know, blunted, if you were a psychic? It just seems like it would be a lot of work all the time."

Charlotte hooted.

"And she kept staring at my shoulder. Or, like, over my shoulder, like we were at a cocktail party and she was looking to see if there was anyone else she'd rather talk to." Leah heard her words as they came out of her mouth and hung in the air between her lips and the cell phone. "Oh god."

"What?" said Charlotte.

"Oh my god." She flipped the phone closed and started to run. She ran as hard as she could until she got home, and then she slammed the door shut.

Leah hadn't been outside since.

. . .

Henry couldn't sleep. It wasn't a bad thing, but it was unusual. Henry could always sleep. But lately, his songs had been waking him up early, nagging him out of bed in the grey light of dawn, hassling him till he had the guitar on his knee, the strings beneath his fingers. I am here, the guitar seemed to call, where are you? The presence of the pigeon in his life, that brief interlude, was like a dream to him now. A strange and magical tide that had risen and then receded, leaving behind a film of happiness and good fortune over everything Henry touched. The songs he was writing were like magic, Dave O'Dell's card on James's bureau was a lucky charm, a magical talisman. He was well and truly free of Tina and ready, so ready, for whatever was coming next. He kept that scrap of paper with its pencil-scratched spell on it taped to the side of his guitar, crowning the list of songs that was growing every few days. It was all going Henry's way. And it was about time.

He ran his fingers over the strings, loved the sweet sound they made with so little effort on his part. An old favourite to get started, he decided. The song had been in his head for weeks now. He couldn't explain it and he didn't care. He leaned back in the little rocking chair, opened his mouth and sang.

. . .

She awoke in horror. Heart pounding, mouth sere. Nathan, Nathan. It took a moment to realise what morning it was. That the horror was not fresh, though it felt so. That he'd been missing for three weeks. That she was the one who could help him, except that once again, she'd chosen to stay home.

The phone rang and Leah shifted in the bed. She didn't feel like speaking with anyone. There were only a few people it could be, anyhow. Charlotte maybe, or maybe Laurie at *Bite This* with an assignment or a question. The phone rang four times, then stopped. Leah stretched glumly, then checked the voicemail.

"This is an automated message from the Halifax Regional Public Library system," a robotic voice said. "You have one overdue book. The book is called"—and here another voice broke in—"'How To Deal With Ghosts' by Peter Pietropaulo." The robotic voice returned. "Please return this book to any branch of the Halifax Regional Public Library system at your earliest convenience. Thank you."

Leah clicked off the phone and wished she could as easily click off the dreams that still lurked at the back of her mind. Stupid Pietropaulo and his stupid book. What good had it been to her? Here she was, worse off than she'd been the day she borrowed the damn thing. No closer to freeing Nathan, haunted by bad dreams and now she'd have to pay a stupid overdue fine, too. She didn't even know where the book was. Last she'd seen it, Charlotte was reading it by flashlight. Maybe Charlotte had it. She dialed her friend.

"Nah," said Charlotte. "I left it at your place, on the floor. It probably got kicked under the chair. Fascinating stuff, though. Especially the part about why ghosts hang around."

"Oh yeah?" Leah said.

"Yeah dude. The four main reasons—I don't know where the guy gets that stuff, but it's sure a good read."

"Four main reasons?" Leah asked, her heart dropping.

"Yeah, didn't you read that part?"

"Not exactly," Leah said. Her mouth went dry for the second time that morning. "I kind of skipped right to the part about how to get rid of your ghost. I just figured Nathan was here because, I don't know. Because he didn't know where he was supposed to be."

"Huh," Charlotte said. "Well, the guy says that's the case for some ghosts, but it's not like Nathan's death was a surprise to him. Could he have had some unfinished business?"

"I doubt it," Leah said. She felt sick. "He was pretty methodical. Had everything sewn up and taken care of."

"Could he be feeling guilty?" Charlotte asked.

Leah pulled both lips in over her teeth, her mouth a thin line.

"Guilty about leaving everyone?" Charlotte prodded.

"Maybe," Leah said, her voice small. "It wouldn't be totally out of character." But something told her it wasn't Nathan's guilt that was keeping him here.

"I think you'd better find that book," Charlotte said. "And read the rest of it."

"Yeah," Leah said.

Leah leapt out of the bed as if it was filling with water, and pulled on dirty jeans and a turtleneck from the floor. She flew down the stairs, almost tripping over Neil in her haste.

In the living room, she scrabbled under the chair Charlotte had sat in during the power-out. In the dim under-chair light, through the haze of cat-hair tufts, she saw the book. She pulled it out, its green cover dulled by dust and neglect. She rubbed it on her jeans and flipped through it hastily, till she found the section she was looking for.

Why do ghosts stay on earth? she read. Sometimes, ghosts don't know they are ghosts. Perhaps their death was sudden or unexpected. The afterlife can be tremendously confusing, and if the quietus came in the form of a speeding bus, a violent murder, an avalanche or hurricane, for instance, the spirit may have no idea that he or she is dead. They may have no idea what to do, how to behave, where to go. And so they continue to hang around. They often stay very near the place where their death occurred.

Ghosts will also stay earthbound if they feel they have unfinished business. This may include family matters or financial issues they did not have a chance to clear up before their death. They will stay on earth as long as they need to in order to square things away to their satisfaction. They will occasionally, if the task is complicated, attempt to enlist human help. This sometimes makes the task take longer to complete, as the ghost is only able to communicate in metaphors. For reasons that are not yet clear to spectral realm researchers, spirits eschew direct contact.

The third reason spirits may decide not to go on is human guilt. The spirit may itself feel guilty, may feel it has left loved ones in the lurch. In this case, spirits will stay on earth and attempt to look after the family left behind. By the same token, if it is a loved one who cannot let go of the deceased, the spirit will wait, sometimes for years, until their loved ones are ready to let go.

Leah's head snapped up. Recognition coursed through her like an electrical current. It was her. It was because of her. She paged clumsily through the book to the section she had read not quite enough of in the first place.

How can I get rid of my ghost? She devoured the words. She'd read it before—she thought she'd read the pertinent parts. She'd been following its advice all this time. But clearly, she'd missed something.

There are many ways to help a spirit find its way to the light, Pietropaulo had written. In the case of a spirit who does not know he or she has passed, you will have to actually tell the spirit his or her story—in effect, you will have to break to them the news of their passing. This will be no easy task—remember, spirits do not respond to direct contact! You will have to find an indirect way to communicate. You may perhaps choose to tell the ghost's story to someone nearby—that may be enough to help your spirit move along.

If you do not know the spirit and do not wish to have further contact with it, simply hold up your hands in front of your face and say, firmly but kindly, NO. This will not likely help the spirit move on to the light, but it will help it move on, perhaps to find someone who can escort it to the next world.

Leah had stopped reading there. It was stuff she already knew, she'd felt. That information about how to get a ghost to stop visiting you, the holding up the hands. Everyone knew that. So she hadn't pushed on any further in the book. She shook her head, impatient with her own impatience. Tears were starting to burn at the back of her eyes, but she willed them away. No time for that now. She had to figure out what she'd been doing wrong, and set it right. If Nathan was still here because of her, she had to make amends.

If you are the reason a ghost is hanging around, the chapter continued, if you suspect your ghost may be feeling guilty about leaving you, or if you are having trouble letting go of your loved one, you must find a way to prove to the ghost that you are alright, and then he or she will be able to move toward the light.

Leah slammed the book shut, slinked into her jacket and banged out the door before she could think before she could let her guilt keep her inside one minute longer. She felt flayed, as she ran down the street, book in hand, to be out in the daylight, in the mild busyness of a Sunday morning in the north end of town. Still, she had to get there, had to get to the library in case it wasn't too late. She ran.

. . .

Nathan paced. He sniffed the air. It was possible something was about to change, but it was also possible that that something was simply the weather. He prayed there'd be no rain. Well, that was different. He never used to pray. But things aren't what they were, he told himself. That much was abundantly clear. He went to stand near Winston Churchill. Folded his arms behind his back and strolled the path. It felt alright. He preferred his arms down, but Winston had a point. He did feel calmer, more leader-ish with his arms tucked away neatly like that. He practised, and he waited.

. . .

Leah ran. She never ran, but she ran now. She panted, her hair flew around her face, she began to sweat all over and her ankles threatened to crumple at every turn, but still she ran. She thought about running up Citadel Hill, but that would just slow her down, so she ran around it instead, and then, feeling panic pushing her faster than she'd known she could go, she ran down the dip it made in her city, a dip that took her right to the library. She didn't know what too late would be, she only hoped she wouldn't have to find out. She wasn't sure she'd be able to see Nathan or feel him. Didn't matter. She knew what she had to do now, and she would just do it, and not worry about the outcome. If it worked, it worked. If not—"If not, I'll feel guilty forever, which I was going to do anyhow. So no big deal," she panted.

She cruised down the hill to the library, slowing her pace so she wouldn't be too out of breath when she got there. The library was quiet this morning, thank god, she thought. What she was going to do was weird enough—she didn't need an audience. She looked around. It wasn't quite true. She did need an audience, an audience of one, but she didn't see him there. "Shit, goddamn," she said, catching her breath. Well, whatever. She'd already decided she was going to do it whether she saw him or not, and here she was, so she'd better get started. She sat on the steps, put her hands on her knees. In the absence of strangers to be seeming to tell the story to, she just launched in and told it to herself, out loud, in the hopes that Nathan would overhear and realise.

"Okay, with Nathan, it's like this," she said. "When he first was sick, I didn't believe it. Couldn't believe it. He was a vegetarian! He never smoked—except for that one pack of Colts, those wine-tips, when he was in first year. But other than that, no, he hated that shit. So it didn't seem reasonable that he could be sick like that. I didn't even believe it when I saw him, like a skeleton in overalls. And he was smiling. It was unreal. Then he got better, and he and Rebecca seemed so happy and I just kind of put it out of my mind. And I only saw him a few times a year, but he always looked good to me, and he said he was fine, and I wanted to believe him and I believed him.

"Then a year went by and he got sick again. And I went home to see him, and he was so thin, with an IV port in his arm, but he pretended it was normal, and I didn't want to spook him, so I pretended too. And he seemed stressed out, but I, oh, it's not that I didn't notice, but I guess I didn't know what to do with it. And Mom and Dad were freaking out and Rebecca was totally freaking out, and everyone was just so upset, that I got back on a plane and flew home to Halifax just as fast as I could. And then he went under the knife again and it was no good. It was no good, and everyone was crying on the phone, but Dad said he wasn't going to die and I should stay put, so I did." She swallowed. It was not easy. But it was necessary. And she'd been taking the easy way out for some time now. It wasn't making her happy and it wasn't helping Nathan. She swallowed again. It felt absurd to be talking to no one, but absurdity was becoming commonplace to Leah.

"And you know what? I called all the time that fall, while he was 'convalescing'. I called all the time, but I never spoke to him and I rarely asked how he was. I just didn't know the words, you know? I spend my time with all these words, but when it came to him, that fall, I didn't have a single one."

Leah gulped, looked around wildly, still saw no one. She drew a deep breath, went back in.

"Christmas," she said, staccato. "I went home and cried. I cried at the Santa's Village at the mall with Mom. I cried in church on Christmas Eve. I cried every time I looked at Dad, so finally I learned not to look at him. I dreaded the moment Nathan would arrive. When he did, he was a stick," she said flatly. "He was a bony old man with big black eyes and giant loops of dirty hair that stuck up all over his head in tufts where the chemo had left it alone. He moved like a board and he talked to his girlfriend like they were both two years old and fighting over a toy in the sandbox. He went to the hospital every second day. Finally, they told him no food. Two days before Christmas. We went crazy. He didn't talk. I couldn't talk to him. He ate a shred of turkey and threw-up violently in the sink. I was there, but I didn't even hold his hand. Too stupid to know how to."

Leah was crying by now, taking great heaving breaths, but she had to press on.

"February. I went home for Mom's birthday. 'Doesn't Nathan look good?' I kept saying, 'I think he looks really good' No one had the heart to tell me I was an idiot, that Nathan was on his way out a bit more every day. And though I noticed that all of us crowded into one corner to eat so that he wouldn't see us, though I noticed that as he sat, he clenched his fists and glared at his lap, I talked to him about nothing. Or worse, I didn't talk to him at all."

A figure emerged from behind Winston Churchill. It flickered in and out like a radio with bad reception.

"April," she practically shouted. "He called to say he'd gone off his chemo for good. It's not helping he told me, and in fact, it's making me sicker. He told me how he might die, that basically his organs would fail. Should I come home, I said. I'm not going to die tomorrow he said, so stay where you are. He was so matter of fact about it. I didn't even ask him how he felt. Instead, we talked about my job." She looked around, but couldn't see him anymore. She was almost there—she was almost done. At least she knew he'd heard some of it.

"May," she said, sorrowfully. "He went into the hospital for tests, and instead he got pneumonia. They had to put him in a coma so they could stick tubes down his throat so he could breathe. I came home a day too late. One day earlier, his morphine dose was low enough he could still smile, respond, blink. By the time I got home he was deep inside. His feet were huge, greenish, swollen. His hands, too. He smelled weird. He was hooked up to machines, surrounded by nurses. I sat beside him for hours, holding his hand, the way I never did when he was—the way I never did before. I talked to him then, but not out loud, just in my head, as if he was already dead, as if he could read my mind. The nurses said he could hear me if I talked, but I couldn't talk. I could only think. Stupid thoughts." She looked down at the ground, her voice barely above a whisper.

"He died in the night. They said Rebecca was with him, and she never said she wasn't, but I've always thought she got there a minute too late. I don't know why. We missed him by ten. His skin was still warm. When I saw the machines turned away, I thought for a moment he must be better. Oh good, I thought. And then quickly, no, not good. We'd been with him a few hours before, just us, me and Mom and Dad. And we were laughing and horsing around in his room, and he was breathing hard, trying to take over from the respirator machine, the way he did that week, whenever there was action in his room, whenever we were all there, talking and laughing and telling stories about him, the way we did. And we were thinking about spending the whole night with him, but then we thought maybe it would tire him out, stress him out to have us there. So we left. We said we'd see him the next day and we left. And then he was gone. He died."

Leah flung the tears from her eyes, drew a tremendous breath into her lungs and looked up. Nathan stood there.

"And it was awful," Leah said slowly. "It was so awful, Nathan. And it still is, every day."

His skin was warm and brown, his eyes were big and black and they looked at her kindly.

"But this is how it is," she said quietly. "We have to try to be alright with it."

He looked directly at her, he looked deep into her eyes for just a moment, her heart jumped in her chest at the sight of him, and then he put one hand up and faded away.

Leah sat for a while on the steps of the library. She'd never said all that out loud before. It felt, not good exactly, but necessary. And that would do for now. She got to her feet. The hip-hop kid was coming down the path.

"Hey," she said.

"Hey," he said, "do they still do free food here on Sunday afternoons?"

"I think so," she said. "But not for a few hours yet. You

okay?"

"Yeah," the kid said. "I'll just wait." And he sat on the steps where she'd been moments before.

She nodded at him and turned for home.

She thought the city would feel different, but it didn't, it felt just the same. It smelled a bit like imminent spring, but that could just be the ocean playing tricks. She'd definitely been fooled before. The skin on her back felt warm and tingly under her coat. It was a friendly kind of tingle, a kind of prickling excitement, the kind you got when you were going to home, to see people you hadn't in too long. She kicked her feet through the slush on the sidewalks and thought about meatballs. She bet there'd be plenty of those tonight.

There were dogs out on the Common, but there were always dogs. Their people stood in clumps, their hands in their pockets clutching empty plastic bags at the ready. No, Leah was definitely more of a cat person. Just one more thing Psychic Sue had gotten wrong. Well, it didn't matter. She knew what she needed to know, for now, and that was good enough for her.

. . .

Henry tipped his head back and sang for all he was worth, sang like he hadn't sung in more weeks than he could count. His wide mouth turned up in an everlasting smile as the music poured out. He felt full of it, suffused with it, with light, with the tune, he wished he could climb inside its individual notes, live inside there, understand it from within. As soon as he got to the end, he thought, he'd start again from the beginning.

. . .

She sauntered along through the Common not wanting the walk to end. She kept expecting the clouds to break and the blue sky to come through, and those rays of light that shone down through the clouds from time to time and to look like God. She expected all of that, but she wasn't particularly surprised when it didn't come. The sky stayed solid grey as it had for weeks, and as it would, no doubt, continue to. Till the day it stopped doing that and did something else instead. Things can be one way one minute, Leah thought, and then entirely another way the next. It wasn't the first time she'd thought that, mind you, but it was the first time she'd thought it without fear. She wrapped her arms around herself and gave a little squeeze.

She could hear the music before she even got to the street. It spilled out into the morning's grey light. She had cried all she was going to cry, for the day, at least. She stopped just short of her own front door and knocked.

. . .

The hip-hop kid sat on the library steps. It was getting warmer out, and he didn't mind waiting. He hadn't seen the birds for a while—since the day he'd written back, as a matter of fact—and he guessed that meant the end of that bit of income. That figured. But it was okay—One-Eyed Carl was back from Montréal, and he'd started a new venture. Some kind of bike courier company. He'd told the kid he'd have work for him starting in a week or two. So it seemed like everything was going to be alright after all. The kid patted his parka pockets, looking for a cigarette. He found a slightly crumpled one and a lighter and he sat on the steps and smoked.

. . .

Henry heard the knock and was surprised. It wasn't like Parker to just drop by, and anyhow it was indecently early on a Sunday morning. No way the guy was even out of bed. He wondered who else it could be, realised there was no answer for that and thought, damn, I have got to get out more, see more people. Probably someone trying to sell him something. Or a Jehovah's Witness. Who would, he reasoned, also be trying to sell him something. Reluctantly, he put the guitar down and went to the door.

She had long black hair that curled over her shoulders and big grey eyes in a heart-shaped face. He'd never seen her before in his life.

"Sorry," he said, smiling politely. "James and Emily are away."

"I know," she said. "I live next door."

"Ah," Henry said. Here came the downer to his day. What a shame. "Sorry. Was I making too much noise?"

She smiled. "You could use a lighter hand on the door slamming, that's for sure. But no, the music is—the music is fine."

They stood and looked at each other. Finally, Henry gestured to the hallway. "Would you like to come in?"

She nodded. "I'd like that, yeah."

He stepped back to let her in. She stood in the hallway and took off her coat, slid her feet out of their shoes. They looked at each other for an awkward beat.

"Um, can I take your coat?" Henry asked. He wished he

knew just what was happening here. Who was this woman, and what did she want? "Would you like some coffee?"

"Sure," she said. "That would be great." She held out her jacket. "I'm Leah," she said.

"Leah," Henry repeated. "Nice to meet you." He hung her coat on the banister's newel post. "Henry."

"Hi, Henry," Leah said shyly.

"Hi," he said. "Okay. Coffee. This way."

He headed down the hallway to the kitchen; she followed.

"Have you eaten?" he asked over his shoulder. He didn't know why, but he wanted to take care of her. She was so open, somehow. It made him want to do things for her.

"Oh," she said. "No, not yet. But don't worry about that. I don't want to take you away from whatever you're doing." She spotted the guitar leaning against the wood stove. "Whoops," she said, "don't want to leave that there for too long." She moved it over, leaned it against the wall instead. "Nice guitar," she said.

"Do you play?"

"No," she said. "I just admire the ability in others."

"Here," he said, holding out a mug of coffee. "What do you take?"

"Nothing," she said. She sat at the kitchen table.

Henry leaned against the counter and looked at her. She seemed so at home. As if they'd agreed to have coffee together. As if she were absolutely where she was meant to be.

She sipped her coffee, looked up at him over the rim of her cup. "Everything okay?" she asked.

"Yeah," he said. "Everything's okay. Everything's great."

"Good," she said.

"Good," he repeated. He sipped his coffee.

. . .

Charlotte woke up, rolled toward Johnny Parker in the bed. She kissed his collarbone until he woke. "Good morning," she murmured into his skin.

"Good morning," he agreed.

"You know who'd like Henry," she mumbled into his stubble.

"Many people would," he allowed, yawning a little. "Henry is a very likeable fellow."

"Leah would like him," Charlotte said. "That's who."

"That so," said Johnny. "I never figured you for a matchmaker."

"I'm not," Charlotte said. "I just think they'd really like each other."

"You're just a big sook," Johnny said. "And you want everyone else to be as big a sook as you." He yawned again. "I could sleep for ten years," he said and closed his eyes.

. . .

Henry couldn't stop himself. He told Leah all about the songs he'd been writing, and about Dave O'Dell, and his plans for the future. "This guy really likes my songs," he said. "I think he's going to help me out."

"That's great," Leah said. She was on her second cup of coffee. "Well, they sound good through the wall."

Henry swallowed and felt the redness rise in his face. "You can hear me through the wall?"

Leah grinned. "Yeah."

Henry squeezed his eyes shut. Leah laughed.

"It's okay," she said. "You sound good. And you always

warm up with my favourite song. Though for a while I thought I was going mad because I kept hearing it."

"Oh yeah?" Henry said, glad to have the focus off himself for a minute.

"Yeah," Leah said. She looked at him, considering. "Yeah. This psychic I know told me that when I heard that song, it was my brother playing it for me." She squinted one eye, took a deep breath and sized up the situation. "He used to play it for me all the time." She blew on her coffee. "When he was alive."

Henry raised his eyebrows. "Really," he said. "Huh."

"Wow," Leah said. "I sound crazy. But I'm not, actually."

"Okay," Henry said. "It's okay."

She passed a hand over her eyes and grimaced like she was in pain. "Gah. So embarrassing."

"No," said Henry. "Not at all. I mean, listen, a bird changed my life. Talk about embarrassing."

She opened her eyes. "A bird, you say."

"Homing pigeon type bird," Henry confirmed. "It just flew in here one day and wouldn't leave. It had a message on its leg for me and everything." He saw the look on her face and thought she disbelieved him. "Well," he amended, "I don't know for sure it was for me, but then, the bird wouldn't leave, so what was I to think? It just hung out right here," he tapped the counter, "for two or three days. Flew around the house whenever I played the guitar, but otherwise, just sat here and ate mashed up crackers. Cute little guy," he said, "once I got used to him."

"And then what?" Leah asked urgently.

"Then one day he was gone," Henry said. "But I kept the note."

"Let me see it," she said. "Where is it?"

"Right here on my guitar." He pulled it onto his knee, turned its side toward Leah. "See? It says I am here, where are you."

Leah sat back in her chair, the wind knocked out of her.

Henry kept talking, the sentences coming in a rush. "I still have no idea who it's from or what it means. But it woke me up. And everything changed after that."

"I know who sent it," she said, a funny look in her eye. Henry raised his eyebrows again. "I know exactly who it's from." She looked at him. He shrugged as if to lure the story out of her.

"It's a long story," she said.

"I'm not going anywhere," he said.

Leah opened the fridge. "Is all this yours? Can I use anything I like? I suddenly feel super hungry."

. . .

Johnny Parker awoke to the smell of coffee. "Darlin'," he called from the bedroom, "you're just about the best thing that's ever happened to me."

"Well, duh," Charlotte called back.

. . .

Leah cooked and talked and sipped her coffee. It felt good to tell the whole story to someone who didn't know her at all. She whisked eggs and steamed spinach and chopped an onion. She rooted around in the fridge and found a jar of artichokes hiding at the back. She chopped them and threw them in the pie plate along with the rest of the ingredients. "Do you have a pepper-grinder?" she asked, interrupting herself. Henry pointed her towards a giant wooden grinder. She cranked it over the pie plate and popped the whole thing in the oven.

She sat down again at the table and said "it'll be ready in about fifteen minutes." She swallowed some coffee.

"So?" Henry asked impatiently.

"So," Leah said. "I realised what was holding Nathan here. It wasn't that he didn't know he was a ghost. It was me. And all those notes I sent by pigeon-post, who knows what happened to them. I don't think it matters. Obviously, someone received them." She gestured toward the note taped to his guitar. "Soon as I figured out that the problem was with me, that was all it took. I ran down to the library and spilled my guts."

"Did it work?" Henry asked.

"I don't know," Leah said slowly. "I saw him, for a minute, and then he faded away."

"And how do you feel?"

"You know," she said, "I feel the way I did when he was with me. I feel safe. But it's more than that. I feel like I'm going to be okay. It might take a while, but in the end, I'll be alright." She nodded. "Yeah."

Henry nodded too. He picked up his guitar again, tuned it and started to play. Leah smiled at the familiar chords. They always made her cry, but this time, she didn't think she would. She felt a hand on the top of her head, warm and comforting. And then she felt it lift, and leave, and that was okay too. She watched Henry as he bent over his instrument, his fingers deftly moving over the strings. He lifted his head and was about to sing. Leah smiled at him broadly. He smiled back, hugely, a giant smile the likes of which she'd never seen, closed his eyes and started to sing.

. . .

Nathan held up his plate and called across the room, "Is there any more?"

"There's plenty more," Noni said. She smiled at her grandson and ran her hand through his thick curly hair. "What else do you want?" she asked.

"Whatever you've got," he said, handing her his plate.

ACKNOWLEDGEMENTS

Ah, the acknowledgements, cherished friend to novelists during times of writers' block and wavering faith. Speaking of such things, Suzanne Matczuk gave me a stern talking to, endless support and encouragement, and the notion of homing pigeons over an excellent supper at an Ethiopian place in Winnipeg, and for that, I thank her. Thanks also to the writers' group in Winnipeg, my first readers, who were kind and gentle people, especially when it came to my super rough first draft. Meagan Perry and Iris Yudai smilingly put up with much obsessive word counting and plot-discussion. Huge thanks to Chris Boyce and all my former colleagues at DNTO for letting me experiment with this book on their radio show. And thanks to the fierce women of HEN, whose love of books and chatter kept me warm for two long winters.

Thanks to Andrew Kaufman—my fifth business—Tom Barkhouse and Andy Pedersen (who dreamed I wrote novels).

Thanks to Jane Buss and everyone at the Writers' Federation of Nova Scotia for always making me feel like a writer, even when I was having trouble putting my fingers on the keyboard. Thanks especially to Sue Goyette, who showed me that how I take a bath is how I take a bath, and that it's alright either way. And that it's completely normal to hate rewriting. My fellows in the Fiction Marathon 06-07, helped me figure out what the holy hell I was doing, anyhow. The Halifax writers' group of Sue Carter Flinn, Sean Flinn, Anthony Black, Carsten Knox, Robin Lathrop, Camille Fouillard, Ryan Turner and Sarah Mian reeled me in and kept me from flopping all over the boat.

Shayla Howell took my cranky mood in stride for more months than you can imagine, and when things were really falling apart, she helped put them back together. Her relentless relentlessness helped me fix my book's shaky logic to the best of my abilities. Where it falls down is my problem, not hers. But her help cannot be understated.

By this time you may well be wondering if I did any of this myself, and hey, that's a great question.

Carmen Klassen, Janet Irwin, Susan Mitton and all my colleagues at CBC Halifax are just the right blend of curious and supportive.

Robbie MacGregor is a fine person to eat strawberries with in the backyard in summer, especially if you're a writer, because he's given to saying lovely things like, I think I'd like to publish your book. Sacha Jackson and I have never met, but she edited this sucker as if she'd been there from the start.

Carmie Domet taught me to love reading, and how to hold a pencil to form letters. And then later, she gave me my first piece of critical advice. Plus, there was that whole thing where she gave birth to me and all. Ray Domet gave me part of his poet's soul, and the good sense to buy canned food when it's on sale with the happy result that when you're writing, there's always something to have for supper. Chris, Jeff and Donna Domet gave me a lifetime of unstinting friendship. Em, Sofia and Veronica, Michelle and Emily: a finer gaggle of girls it is hard to imagine. And thanks must also go to Piccolos, Domets, Zahers, Sheriffs, Stephens and Longos all of whom have shaped me, and especially Aunt Laura.

Johnny Parker, here's your legacy. Thanks for making me laugh my ass off, and thanks for not suing me.

And then there's Kev. Whom I love and adore, whom I'd do anything for. Whose Cheshire Cat grin is all I need. And who shows me every day what it is to love someone.

A NOTE FROM THE PUBLISHER

Invisible Publishing is a not-for-profit publishing company that produces contemporary works of fiction, creative non-fiction, and poetry. We publish material that's engaging, literary, current, and uniquely Canadian. We're small in scale, but we take our work, and our mission, seriously. We produce culturally relevant titles that are well written, beautifully designed, and affordable.

Invisible Publishing has been in operation for just over half a decade. Since releasing our first fiction titles in the spring of 2007, our catalogue has come to include works of graphic fiction and non-fiction, pop culture biographies, experimental poetry and prose.

Invisible Publishing continues to produce high quality literary works, we're also home to the Bibliophonic series and the Snare imprint.

If you'd like to know more please get in touch.
info@invisiblepublishing.com

Invisible Publishing
Halifax & Toronto

WATERBABY

T0155040

WATERBABY
NIKKI WALLSCHLAEGER

COPPER CANYON PRESS
PORT TOWNSEND, WASHINGTON

Cover art: Courtesy of Nikki Wallschlaeger

Copper Canyon Press is in residence at Fort Worden State Park in Port Townsend, Washington, under the auspices of Centrum. Centrum is a gathering place for artists and creative thinkers from around the world, students of all ages and backgrounds, and audiences seeking extraordinary cultural enrichment.

LIBRARY OF CONGRESS CATALOGING-IN-PUBLICATION DATA
Names: Wallschlaeger, Nikki, author.
Title: Waterbaby / Nikki Wallschlaeger.
Description: Port Townsend, Washington : Copper Canyon Press, [2021] |
Summary: "A collection of poems by Nikki Wallschlaeger"—Provided by publisher.
Identifiers: LCCN 2020047685 | ISBN 9781556596131 (paperback)
Classification: LCC PS3623.A4453 W38 2021 | DDC 813/.6—dc23
LC record available at https://lccn.loc.gov/2020047685

9 8 7 6 5 4 3 2 FIRST PRINTING

COPPER CANYON PRESS
Post Office Box 271
Port Townsend, Washington 98368
www.coppercanyonpress.org

ACKNOWLEDGMENTS

Poems in this book have been published in the following journals, some in earlier forms:

Academy of American Poets Poem-a-Day: "Mosquitoland"

The American Poetry Review: "American Children," "I'd Come Back from the Grave to Celebrate the End of Capitalism"

Apogee: "This Body Keeps the Keys"

Apology: "Ars Poetica on a Twenty-Dollar Bill," "Blue Flame of July," "Cows in the Morning," "Take a Seat"

The Baffler: "Further Notes on the New Reconstruction"

Bennington Review: "Jamais Vu State of Mind"

Boston Review: "Vertical View of a City"

Brick: "Lost in America," "Lullaby"

Chicago Review: "Airport Security Playlist," "People Are Unbearably Docile"

Conduit: "Astral Traveling Got Me F*cked Up," "Fantastic Voyage"

Denver Quarterly: "A Dying Mule Kicks the Hardest," "Notes on the New Reconstruction," "Valley of Things"

Dreginald: "Birthday," "Nobody Special," "Why Do I Feel So Old When I Look So Young"

The Feminist Wire: "Mother of Thousands"

The Georgia Review: "Women Are Doomed to Be the Angels of Love"

The Iowa Review: "Butterfly on a Baby's Head"

The Journal Petra: "Dirt Floor"

Kenyon Review: "William Carlos Williams"

The Literary Review: "The Lunch Counter of Eternal Tears"

Mississippi Review: "Way of the Road"

The Nation: "It's a Daisy"

The Offing: "Anti-Elegy"

On the Seawall: "100-Year Flood"

Poetry: "When the Devil Leads Us Home and Yells Surprise"

PoetryNow: "All Kinds of Fires inside Our Heads"

Rigorous: "Catfish," "Crash Blue Sunday"

Sixth Finch: "Dead to the World Study #1"

Spoon River Poetry Review: "Middle Passage Messaging Service"

Witness: "Just Because We're Scared Doesn't Mean We're Wrong," "Lonely in a Fundamental Way," "Prayer Sonnet"

"This Body Keeps the Keys" also appeared in the anthology *The BreakBeat Poets Volume 2: Black Girl Magic* (Haymarket, 2018). "Mother of Thousands" was included in the anthology *Bettering American Poetry Volume 2* (Bettering Books, 2017). "When the Devil Leads Us Home and Yells Surprise" will appear in *New Poetry from the Midwest 2019* (New American Press).

For Eileen (1928–2017)

Losers, like autodidacts, always know much more than winners. If you want to win, you need to know just one thing and not to waste your time on anything else: the pleasures of erudition are reserved for losers. The more a person knows, the more things have gone wrong.

UMBERTO ECO, *NUMERO ZERO*

When I'm singing blues, I'm singing life.

ETTA JAMES

CONTENTS

3   Nobody Special

7   Middle Passage Messaging Service

9   All Kinds of Fires inside Our Heads

10 This Body Keeps the Keys

12 Dirt Floor

13 Valley of Things

14 Black Woman on a Plane, Twenty-First Century

17 Prayer Sonnet

18 Airport Security Playlist

19 Jamais Vu State of Mind

20 Women Are Doomed to Be the Angels of Love

22 It's a Daisy

24 When the Devil Leads Us Home and Yells Surprise

26 100-Year Flood

28 Notes on the New Reconstruction

30 Way of the Road

33 Vertical View of a City

♦

37 Blue Flame of July

41 Astral Traveling Got Me F*cked Up

42 Dead to the World Study #1

43 William Shakespeare

44 Robert Frost

45 William Carlos Williams

46   Dead to the World Study #2

47   A Dying Mule Kicks the Hardest

♦

51   Why Do I Feel So Old When I Look So Young

55   American Children

56   Dead to the World Study #3

57   The Lunch Counter of Eternal Tears

58   Fantastic Voyage

59   Dead to the World Study #4

60   Lost in America

61   People Are Unbearably Docile

♦

65   Crash Blue Sunday

69   I'd Come Back from the Grave to Celebrate the End of Capitalism

71   Butterfly on a Baby's Head

72   Cows in the Morning

74   Lake Come and Gone

75   Lonely in a Fundamental Way

76   Further Notes on the New Reconstruction

78   Catfish

79   Just Because We're Scared Doesn't Mean We're Wrong

80   Mosquitoland

82   All Dogs Go to Heaven

83   Black Woman in a Bathtub, Twenty-First Century

84 Anti-Elegy

86 Take a Seat

87 Lullaby

88 Birthday

89 Ars Poetica on a Twenty-Dollar Bill

91 Mother of Thousands

93 *About the Author*

WATERBABY

Nobody Special

Pick up my candles and dust them
I don't know when the spirits get in
housework is done by nobody special
that's the way it's always been

Been working since I was a babe
I come home now and work for free
housework is done by nobody special
that's the way it's always been

I'm nobody special, nobody special
a washerwoman serving the cream
homemade confetti ready for them
playing with what they think of me

I'm nobody special, nobody special
seamstresses weaving our chains
no day off in a month of Novembers
busy making overalls for your gain

Dress up my candles and light them
I have a long long night ahead of me
housework is done by nobody special
that's the way it's always been

Been working before I was born
mother waiting on tables with me
housework is done by nobody special
that's the way it's always been

I'm nobody special, nobody special
waiting for some answers tonight
hoping somebody will hear me out
while the light keeps flickering, flickering

Middle Passage Messaging Service

for Wanda Coleman (1946–2013)

A word is an old story. One word, many stories,
one body, many bodies. To this day they move
across our line break lives & before we are
archived, lungs crackle with smoke until words
form in the long struggle smuggled on impact,
a thunderstorm bites & my world is a prayer
with a moon & all the birds from way back but
my throat is a blue cache of contraband winds,
when it's brutal please help keep our language
thriving on big mama river is the word *maroon*.
Forbidden trees storages of lives pressed page
flowers herbs in their barbarian jailships on the
horizon bones shake with births & coughing,
keeping it down catching sick on the landform.
In life I live in the cold foliage of their unreason,
walking pneumonia drowned stories struggle,
silent memoirs, the cooking stoves are loaded
on the horizons cargo & people to this day
they run the sea months mouths housetraps.
Tearin the roof off this cold cruel mothafucka
outside the towers of excess is fluid smoking,
language tundra rumbling running ear nose
& throats tarsus tomes winking out of their
power plants, good & plenty different worlds
tearjerkers crybabies they got no memories
of their own cruelty waterlogged lifesickness.
To cry so hard is to laugh to laugh so hard
is to cry writing with the smoke is the word,
is an old story of our lives of the horizons in my
mouth, I bite the stories that drowned me in

their books with a moon & our real stories.
We live within the fugitivity of a thunderstorm,
lung-red caches formed from struggle from
walking from counting the siq seas mouthing
directions the language cargo of Black code.
We got all the words for how we got here,
where we are going & how we will get there.

All Kinds of Fires inside Our Heads

The number of bodies I have
is equal to the number of
gurney transfers that are
televised.

If we're all "just human"
then who is responsible?

A fire station drying out
from addiction. Outside
the drizzling of firepower,
lowballing suns.

It's like a sauna in here,
the strain of a charred
bladder. Bottled water,
bad wiring.

That spark is no good.
Come sit with me for a
minute. My feet full of
diluted axe fluid.

Thought I heard you say
everything is medicine.
But that's just hearin
what you wanna hear

This Body Keeps the Keys

My dear sparkly-eyed polyps,
I don't have enough juice to
be the sole joist of this family
today,

so I dream of claw-foot tubs
where I splash unapologetic
on how deep this umbilical gets
slumped from getting over,

hair unwashed, toenails randy
as hell because I am sincerely
mothered the fuck out, so tired,
this mothering body,

shellac lying facedown on a
coastline ashing & mottled
pockmarked canker sorrel
no good pictures of myself.

Skinbag workhorse bb creamery,
constant upkeep of management
cultivation of self-care cosmetic
Black pride goddess goddamn!

This shit gets tiresome putting so
much effort into what doesn't last,
sometimes I want to retire shave
my head be a nun or a monk,

just so I can forget all the years
time bludgeoned so I could look like
somebody else swimming around
in their own pallid wheel of tears.

Yemaya, what is to become of us.
I drag my body around lovingly but
it still won't let me go

Dirt Floor

for May Ayim (1960–1996)

The overseers are buried aboveground in containers that won't incinerate, and the workers who made the stones to fit their bodies, dead from lung disease, are stalked by the heavy, wet coughs of their bosses.

In the shaky global clay, the coral reefs are dying from pneumonia. My grandfather packed crates of blank tombstones at the granite quarry for a living and the sea being what it is speaks of these connections. I know when I'm being haunted,

I know when I'm being asked. So we search together through the trenches of buried papers, brown women shoveling, worried for the health of our backs. We are a bouquet of spines pressed into the dirt floor, gathered in strength for you, so you can rest here without loneliness.

Valley of Things

Hang your head when you walk

yesterday's news is greener

to survive ham with ideas

of a common holiness

decisions to make about

what's going to siphon

off your thoughts

fuse giddiness to

the citizen elective

creature by creature

when a very young child

throws down an object

it's beautiful to watch

they don't know about

the value of thingification

hanging over the riverbanks

a good poet prays to nature

I brush out tangles during

graceful animal hunting season

sometimes we hear a crush

figure out a daily schedule

read tortured philosophers

listen to James Booker on repeat

Black Woman on a Plane, Twenty-First Century

Minutiae in a bowl,
jury-rigged hand
in need of a drink.

The flight attendant
said, "It's on me,"

I must've looked
like I needed one.

Such a rough climb,
wobbly as the sun
during Leo season.

Come to find out
a brand new plane
is hot to handle.

The first breath,
crucial, coughs.

My favorite path
of looking winds up
when I'm in the air.

There's no way
to vacuum-seal death
up here I suppose,

even though I've never
felt the urge to buy
a traveling pillow.

If something develops,
if our machine defects,

I'll ask if I can hold
the hand of the woman
who gave me a drink.

Then it's time to land
like nothing happened,

the captain standing
at the door with his crew.

He's younger than I am,
a baby-faced white boy.

We don't know his name,
or where he came from.

Prayer Sonnet

Sewn up again in a data harvest meadow

moving through me as pelvic bowl thunder

to learn how to laugh at their indifference

Revenge of the Chattel is not being shown in

the popular gendarme art houses

blood heavy as the iron binding us together

Public wordplay is called getting dragged

Violences of daily metaphor

in our very real world

These solvent metaphors are true

Hell investigates life with great opportunity

My lil candle mouth kindling for the wounded

when the stars are committed to the worst timing

& no one wants to get out of bed in the morning

Airport Security Playlist

1. Losing My Religion R.E.M.

2. Somebody Blew Up America Amiri Baraka

3. Jonesed Wanda Coleman

4. Without a Face Rage Against the Machine

5. Crazy Nigger Julius Eastman

6. Ghetto Bird Ice Cube

7. Thoughts Green Velvet

8. Everybody Knows Leonard Cohen

9. Everybody Hurts R.E.M.

10. Nobody Cares Deborah Cox

11. Let's Go Get Stoned Big Mama Thornton

Jamais Vu State of Mind

When you keep repeating a lie
people will accept it as truth.
But underneath that feeling is a
merciful border that never existed,
splitting the familiar stone tablets
when we grind our teeth at night
& wake up in the morning tired.
There's a lot of work to get done,
love & devotion are strange deities
who are notoriously indirect with
their instructions. It happens when
you focus on somebody while walking,
the trees straining toward each other
& past the flailing villages made from
our kin.

Women Are Doomed to Be the Angels of Love

This is so true I involuntarily doodle hearts everywhere I go. I sign my letters compulsively with hearts,

dream of disobedient hearts, work with hearts. I eat them. I boil sauces and the tomatoes on my cutting board form a daisy chain heart. My feet are bound in red ballet slippers,

Lisa Frank–style, engorged with crusty satin hearts. I pronounce my name with an embarrassingly hearty accent. My colostrum pools with the plumping of an inflamed heart,

inspired by the nutritional needs of my babies. Hearts are spray-painted on trains like talismans, guiding me eventually to the Heart Afterlife where my treasured friends exist in heart time,

drinking wine and organizing a workers' collective named Heavenly Valley Emotional Workers in the mossy hidden Heart Clouds where my restless heart tires of hearing famous singers

singing sweetly about unsatisfying love in the grocery store when their hearts could be screaming about environmental devastation and global capitalism;

the way this callous dorm pillow I saw online plastered with hearts and dream catchers says "only good vibes" is in no way related to what the hearts of this country really need.

On good days I submit to being a committed student of the heart. On bad days I am paranoid and anxious about my heart being kidnapped by intruders in blue uniforms,

and how a scene in *Indiana Jones and the Temple of Doom* where
the sacrificial victim's heart gets ripped out—in one of Hollywood's
stereotypical cinematic presentations of Indigenous culture—

sent me a message about men who are so powerful they could take
what they wanted from my body with their bare hands.

"Where do bad folks go when they die?" asks Kurt Cobain on my
favorite Nirvana album. I replace "folks" with "hearts" and marvel at
the candor of strange smarmy men on TV who want

to be president, who have no clue being part of a community is
different from purchasing investments in a city. My heart is stone sore.
My heart wants to close forever,

to protect me from market combat. But as a woman bred for strength
and openness I lack options. I'm pretty good at the precarious art of
choosing what gets in,

since doom makes a great gatekeeper,
it's rainwater in a vase of roses on a sleeping hero's grave.

It's a Daisy

Bats twin the sky
drowsy from billowing home
to watch *Night Court*.

I, Nikki, as a contemporary
woman, am bound to ask
who's spiraling in the faucet.

If you keep no-lye relaxers
on your hair past the
suggested time frame,

the original crimple pattern
becomes more defiant.
Memories won't comfort me.

Perhaps it's best not to trust
the politics of people who
haven't washed their own
dishes in twenty years.

O missile management,
I request a transfer 4 the masses
a happy howling cocktail showing

instead of telling this country
That. I. Cannot. With. You.
A freed daylight may be possible,

the revolt in us, I mean. Stems
are still holding like a grown-up
but they snap. You pick me up,

pour me another bath, a glass
of something dry for the blisters,
read Ted Joans's Hand Grenades,

remember that
I'm not the only one and cry.

When the Devil Leads Us Home and Yells Surprise

Is that your house he asked

This used to be my house I said

But those are not your people

So that can't be your house

But it is my house I said

I had some people maybe a few

Even though those are not your people

Even though they don't look like you

I had to live somewhere I said

This is the house where I lived

But where are your people he said

My people live in a different house

They don't care to know about me

If you're the devil

Why are you asking me questions

The devil said since the house

You had to live in is gone

I thought you'd be happy

It sure is a hot day I said

Of course it is said the devil

Why do you think I work in town

100-Year Flood

A barn owl teases the bright dark,
and you are unmanageable.
The people of the area have a
standby way to talk about it,
a right to ferment content
that's forever pushing guidelines
on how to guillotine the poor.
Buildings unhinged and running,
mud tickling through synaptic bricks.
Not sure what we can say
except to repeat the obvious,
and some aren't ungrateful
for an interruption. Disaster brings
lemon pepper frogs and antsy canines,
plenty of puffy men eager to drape
their hero-pose tendons.
I feel satiated by their confidence,
or at least its familiar performance.
An elderly woman told a volunteer
fireman she was too old to care.
What happens when you
struggle for generations
and a storm ejects what you're
still struggling for? In the end

infrastructure owned her,

shelter remained temporary

yet seductive. She refused to patch

her excitement while she reported

on the damage. Decades of keeping

house, children, and working shit jobs

unsettled her more than a

flood ever could.

Notes on the New Reconstruction

The stockroom only the cooks know. Bone bloc broth
commiserating in plain view waters the climbing roses.

Plantations are prisons & prisons produce plantations,
how our runaway slave feet gotta close-read the tides.

Ona Judge is in the West Wing hiding a pistol under the
floorboards. My gods are always horrified by the living,

but she say it's better the devil you know than the devil
you don't. Perfecting their shiny shambolic tapestries,

highly sophisticated ontological equipment cutting
the gooseflesh of a bacon-wrapped fig inside a pig,

rabid glory schemes narrated by their best bombastic
hype agency on top of Capitalism Hill, Incorporated.

A country surreptitiously playing itself with well-worn
and well-torn secrets still plays itself.

Homegirl was twenty-two years old when she outwitted him.

No one cares about a past that's supposed to be done.

Way of the Road

I closed my eyes
so I didn't have to
look at it anymore.
When I opened my
eyes again it was still there.
Same raggedy recollections
but I was farther down the road
than the last time I was willing to rest.
The road is an exasperating concept.
I'd get sent to jail if I drove the car
off into a field of ragweed and chicory
but in my mind something resembling
freedom would spark until the highway
patrol came to take me away.
We're tagged at birth with no excuses,
just follow it and swallow the signs.
Once when I was a child
I was eating with my grandmother
at a throwback hamburger joint
when out of the blue someone drove
a car into the side of the building.
Turned out it was an old white man
who had his foot on the gas
pedal instead of the brake.

A cop arrived as we left certain
the mystical fidelity of insurance
would fix everything, the white man
having been born with an excuse.
Today is not an exceptional day.
Almost every car we've passed
is either a truck or an SUV.
I feel ugly looking at them.
When crossing the street one is
advised to look both ways before
moving, this is a lesson we're
required to learn in elementary school.
Another one is never to accept rides
from strangers. Serial killers wait
in the wings of on-ramps
sucking down packs
of energy drinks while
listening to AM radio.
It's rare I can remember
names of officers. Blueberries,
cherries, fruits for the damned.
You need to finish up your blunts
and crotch the weed immediately
when you see one around you.
On the other side of the highway
bags are unpacked, and German

shepherd dogs bark and mildew

over my overstuffed bladder

buried underneath a rest stop.

The past looks to the future

with a portly film over its eye.

A sack of goldfish breaks

in the centerline and when

you get too close it's gone.

Recollections of dashed memories,

or reflections from a new mirage?

Either way the sirens are enlisted

to stare when we don't belong

(and they're right, we don't),

so I close my eyes again

and when I reopen them,

we've arrived at our destination.

It's the grocery store parking lot

and they're having a sale on

end-of-season vegetable starters.

Vertical View of a City

Buildings stake my breath away
needle in a haystack all crumpled
gets in an unmarked car & follows
as usual people are polishing their
caves below & becoming lonelier

To feel important in the world is
as overbooked as it is up here
situated in a heron's-eye window
hazy pressed lead soaking up
coastlines of sands & swamps

If you know me you know the sky
forever remains a nonstop miracle
& so does the opportunity for joy
living on the ground is the problem
there's a higher risk of getting killed

driving cars & as a Black woman
I have to agree on how steel takes
form in the cast of murder weapons

who kill quickly or slowly & no matter

how many honed rocks we throw back

Mama, here comes the sad part: glass

houses get rebuilt, modified to withstand

a good blast & they say we deserve to

die by them if we get in the way

Blue Flame of July

Can't fix what's beyond repair
baby I know the feeling

A broke clock is right twice a day
don't mean I'm gonna be healing

Any fool can make the rules
any fool will follow them

I know in my soul that's right

Blue flame of July got me good
I can't stop the lies

Break me down before I become
the same old fool I used to be

Can't fix what's beyond repair
baby I know the feeling

A broke clock is right twice a day
don't mean I'm gonna be dealing

If a group of fools makes the rules
all the fools will follow them

Why can't we make better rules
watch the biggest fools swallow them

I know in my soul that's righteous

Blue flame of July got us good
we've got to keep it moving

Break us down before we become
even bigger fools than we used to be

Astral Traveling Got Me F*cked Up

It's no wonder, she said. Capitalism got us so fucked up our souls' bodies are half hanging out all the time. Psychiatrists call this "dissociation" and claim a pill is gonna strengthen the bond between body and soul. The workable plastic regulating you and everything else just gets a little harder, that's all. Prettier. Brighter. Then one day you find yourself in a wig shop trying on blond wigs, brandishing yourself as Barbie.

It's kinda like you're a clothesline with no clothes. The whole point is to have clothes hung off it or else it's just a wispy string fed to the air, right? You're naked before the universe. Strung out. Folks from distant planes aren't laughing, they see an opportunity to use your body to tie up other bodies. But if the soul's been hurt long enough you get sick of trying so you leave your life undressed. Detached. I mean it's fine to take a trip, everyone needs a break from reality, but if pain is the only thing keeping your lifeline intact the trips will get more frequent until

Dead to the World Study #1

We were in a small room that was tiled and smelled like chlorine. Facing each other sitting on two identical milking stools. I asked the questions. You knew what I was asking, interrupted. "I just want my fifteen minutes," you said, and shrugged. The interview was over. We walked down to the river and for a moment looked at the water, which was murky with thick green algae. Without saying goodbye you got in and started walking upstream, the current splashing against your legs while from the riverbank I watched you try to hide your struggle. Overhead, a crystal helicopter appeared and piloted your progress, and I could see little helmeted heads in the teardrop windows. Time passed (or what passes for time in a dream).

I saw the new you—what you wanted—your head being fitted for a helmet. They were having trouble with the mouthpiece. But once it was securely fastened, you breathed gratefully.

William Shakespeare

You got that right. You have written the most remembered anti-Semitic play of all time, but not even you could have foreseen the consequences of the stage you helped set. Here are the players, familiar to you even during your time: politicians determining the fate of a people who are receptive to the dangerous fusion when power controls the rights of its cultural thespians. These days and nights I consult tweets on the procedural stages in which public opinion ossifies, and human beings, real and afraid, shift nervously in their assigned seating. Some walk out, and some stay to listen to protest the scripts as bad actors, chameleon-like, cross fire and obfuscate so the sun only sets on their prescriptive deletion. I have to ask at this point if Art is worth the trouble, if your famous authorized plays and poetry were meant to exist in a state of weaponry.

William, you are not above the law. But the law as you knew it and as I know it was never intended to be just. Which leads me to hold Art in a court of underground contempt. All the world's a stage, you said. But you declined to look at what you were capable of. Here we are anyway, watching the familiar agents learning their destined lines.

Robert Frost

Oh, Robert. Go to bed. I know these woods better than you do, and your faithful horse is trying to tell you something. She's cold, weary, famished, and despises the snow. Nevermind the illicit magic of the unknown land—there's a house hidden in your villager friend's woods. A man will get up early to milk the cows at an industrial farm, as the debts he owes pile up faster than the snow. He sleeps beside a sad woman he hasn't made love to in five years. She will get up to make his breakfast, as she does every morning, and allow herself one peppery sigh over a cup of black coffee after he leaves.

It's a hard life out here, Robert. The lake is frozen solid but more than one wife has drowned in it. The locals say sometimes at night you can see brilliant flares hovering over the surface, and there's a rare song spliced through the wind that spooks the dogs. Stay awhile, beloved poet. Or visit us again when our quaint Vermont woods have ceased to beguile you. You'll find many poems buried here in the country dawn.

William Carlos Williams

After I left we hung it in the sky, so everyone can see what Black
women have done for the world. Against our will or not. I discussed
it with the stars and they agreed to hold up the part of me that will
burn the longest, since the labor it took to live down here can never
be repaid. But most people recognize it as a constellation called the
Big Dipper. Anyway, once there was a poet who wrote a famous poem
about everything depending on a broken-down wheelbarrow rusting
in the rain. I think fairly highly of poets and still give them ideas,
and this man was also a doctor. Quiet and thoughtful. When he was
going about his day I whispered about the ugly wheelbarrow I spent a
lifetime with, pushing it back and forth for the fire.

"William," I said, reaching through the wind to grab his ear. He was
walking with a black umbrella and enjoying the mild rain shower.
There was a farmhouse coming up the road with a wheelbarrow in the
front yard. Someone kind had planted red geraniums in it. He slowed
and faced the direction I was pointing, noticing for the first time the
homely little wheelbarrow. Smile lines broke through the slow earth
of his face. Something good was happening, he was sure of it—and so
was I, because I told him.

Dead to the World Study #2

Downstairs was where we distributed and organized the food. Cartons of ungovernable greens, carrots and potatoes, ripe figs, dusky apples. Hungry people were coming in from everywhere so we fed them. It was a big complex that used to be an estate but now was a vibrant place full of life and dignity. Airplanes landed and were able to attach themselves with ease, bringing supplies and visitors. I was happy living there but that day I was on edge. Tonight was the reading, and I was tasked with setting up a dinner for the two touring poets due to arrive in the late afternoon. I left my post and went upstairs to The Tower where the permanent residents lived, passing my friends' quarters along the way. I didn't like these poets. They still associated the liberated mansions with opulence and leisure, even though the state had dissolved a year ago. To be fair they weren't completely oblivious; their enchantment with this place was more gilded irony than anything else—but the general vibe of the duo continued to be stuck in the old language of server and those to be served. I took my time getting ready. When I got to the room where the reading was held, it had already started. The audience was interested, but the poets were annoyed it wasn't standing room only like they were used to. The table was set with our best cutlery and sprays of ranunculus from the gardens. When the reading was finished I was supposed to escort them to the dining area. As I approached they linked arms and looked above our heads for the nearest exit, pretending they didn't see the gathering of people who wanted to break bread in their honor.

A Dying Mule Kicks the Hardest

One kick and her leg shattered into pieces from a cranky, overworked carriage horse chosen for the state holiday procession. A Black man with imperial authority was shaking the hand of a white man who would inherit this imperial authority since his founding father had left him a generous sum in the family will. From the old television mounted in the corner she could watch the cameras panning across their historic embrace, as the emergency room nurse pretended to look the other way, even when she showed documentation that her insurance plan was covered by the federal government.

One kick and the pipe busted over the cervix of the land. An overseer wanted to impress his boss by being tough on crime. He had gotten some ass the night before and felt the strength of his virility as an unconquerable force. At work the next day his hands trembled as he remembered how she screamed for help. Was it the afterglow of his superior prowess or fear that made him fuck up on the job? He watched the crude oil flow painfully into the local watering supply. He scoffed and muttered "women" under his breath before walking back to the supervising station.

One final kick and the feral dog was dead. Euthanized, as they liked to say in the veterinary community. Alfred P. Southwick, dentist and inventor, was very pleased with himself. All those years of digging into the diseased mouths of Buffalo's finest had finally paid off, and the answer to his legacy had been right in front of him the entire time.

He caressed the headrest of the dentist's chair, imagining society's undesirables twitching with electricity. Their deaths would be painless of course, humane even, justice applied quickly with a flick of a switch. He moaned softly at the elegance of such thoughtful civil efficiencies. Modernity would thank him for years to come. Like lightning guided by the gods of Mount Olympus, his name also would be scorched in eternal white, blazing across the sky.

One more kick and the door busted open. She was ready for them, sitting on the couch with a freshly loaded shotgun. Time was pushing her fast to the end of her life, and after forty-plus years of living in that town she had had enough. The land was rightfully hers and they wanted her off it. They wanted to push every Black person out who managed to get a little something for themselves (and it wasn't much) even if they paid their damn taxes and managed to stay out of jail. So what if she managed to power her house by the solar panels she found at a swap meet and learned how to install at home. Or if she refused to send her kids to their trashy school down the street when her daughter came home one day sunk deeply into a hurt she couldn't excavate. She grew almost all her own food and medicine, collected rainwater to drink. Never bothered nobody and yet here they were coming to arrest her since she started teaching other people how to live off the grid, too—folks living right here in town. To hell with their laws. The kids were grown and she had lived a full life; if today proved to be the day of her reckoning, so be it. Her papers were safe with the great radical lawyer. She raised her gun and waited. Aimed. Hadn't she and her people always been waiting? Not today. Not today.

Why Do I Feel So Old When I Look So Young

Why do I feel so old
when I look so young
Have a night of ok fun
& I feel better & younger
refreshed, maybe lovelier
but in the morning
I feel just as old again.

Hey friend, how are you
I see you're young too
around the same age as me.
Look at those folks with their
big boy pens & crooked chairs
they act younger than we do
& our lives are somewhere else
in faces even older than these.

When I was younger
people thought I was older
so they did older-people
things to me said things too
probably why I'm feelin old
while I'm still lookin young

cuz of what older people did
when I was little, should've
known better not to do.

Say friend, I hear you too
things happened to you
that's the way evil goes
lets people do bad things
don't know why that is but
the how is inside the what
tying the ends of the who
maybe we can stop it from
going to the next someone.

Yes it's like that: the could've
the should've & the would've.
If I would've known then what
I know now maybe I could've
got out of the way but I was
too young and now I'm older
outside the what and the who
but still inside the how & the why.
Let me introduce my old-ass self:

How do you do my name is Young

plus the last time I loved w/o fear

American Children

The children across the street are playing with chalk and they take
turns outlining their bodies on the ground. They write their names in
pink, yellow, orange, green, tagging themselves. Two boys are sitting
on the steps with a platoon of action figures. They have a stick of red
chalk and color bloody clouds around these toys designed to resemble
armed men with limitless permanent strength. There are red-winged
blackbirds nearby and they talk all day into the silence, and since it's
only April, you can see their bodies exposed in the bare trees taking
their time for the next cycle. A few days ago there was an armed man
at large camped out in the woods behind my son's school and the FBI
set up a command center to find him, they found him quickly and
the children were safe this time. They know phrases from the stories
they've seen on television and give the tiny toy men dramatic stories
of heroic violent deaths that end in silence. I'm not sure the children
understand what heroism could be, except that it involves weapons
and blood on the ground and sacrifice. One of the first warm spring
weekends and it's normal for children to play with sticks of chalk and
write their names on the plots of concrete where they live, but there are
no innocent landscapes like a giant sun with flowery arms, or a house
with chimneys, or a dog barking bow wow wow, it's just their little
bodies splayed across the asphalt road while they outline each other,
and the strangest thing is none of them are talking or laughing. They
have become so silent and the red-winged blackbirds talk above us of a
world we know nothing about until it comes.

Dead to the World Study #3

Hold a soul close after they're gone. You weren't interested. Gave a half hug wearing your hair curlers and said, "I was just tired." How to mourn without attachment. If suffering is connection, the best responses are movable, right?

I was unable to stand by myself, so I didn't. Then she came by with an armful of rags and said these were your clothes. But you turned your back and I sat on the floor until it was time to go. Yes, I am protesting your fatigue. I took two of your shirts. Not the scraps she brought, but the collared button-ups you wore when you ate your cereal in the morning.

The Lunch Counter of Eternal Tears

Instead of crying on your shoulder I cry on the internet. Instead of crying I make allusions to crying by cherry-picking the subjects. Instead of crying on his shoulder I build a fountain of black amethyst in an artificial square. Instead of crying I ring the bells of a bottomless road. Instead of crying I listen to Roy Orbison's "Crying" because the way he waterfall-sings "crying" feels like a worn leather booth that wouldn't refuse me service. Instead of crying I understand what I'm sacrificing for someone who's long gone. Instead of crying I think of lurid romantic scenarios where I'm not crying and you're the one being insufferable when you think about me. Instead of crying I listen to "Put Your Head on My Shoulder" by Paul Anka and I recognize how some songs are never about deep emotional connections with special people but for getting in the pants of willowy virgins. Instead of crying I put on *Live-Evil* by Miles Davis to smudge the room of 1950s white nonsense. Instead of crying Miles's trumpet screams like the last free lion dying alone in the wilderness. Can I lay my head on your shoulder and cry?

Fantastic Voyage

Partying ain't my strong point anymore. But hey! I got a trunkful of
Florida water and briefings direct from heaven to favor your steps
and if you're feelin like I do watching the birds drop like snow when
they hit the windows—it's no place for a Black woman like you, this
ICE-nation rigmarole where they profess to have hearts of tissue-paper
condolences. Your ship's name is the S.S. *I Told You So*. Ha! Isn't it?
I see those flaring tendrils pop like an old neon light in a South Philly
dive bar. Lookin down for all of Time shakin your pretty head so
everyone can see those thick everlasting roses they call eyelashes. But
when we look up over and into your eyes they know which way the
wind blows. God is gathering his cards on you, girl. Gets all sanguine
when he mentions your name. Anyway, I'm here anytime you need a
lift cuz I know how you feel about what you got to work with down
here. You're so deep you won't even bother with roads, you need an
entire globe of motion to maneuver at will and even then you'll never
be satisfied.

Dead to the World Study #4

Placing a collect call to the heavens or anywhere you choose to sort
down payments of the spirit. What a relief to hear your voice again.
You're not here with me, that's clear. But your new apartment is
sumptuous with wall-to-wall carpeting and elegant sofas the color
of dusk settling in for the night. I can tell by the tone of your voice
I'm interrupting something, but you're glad I called. "We're just
passing around a cheese platter," you say, giggling into a black rotary
telephone. Wherever you live now you're the hit of the neighborhood.
Everyone wants to come by just like they did on Earth except it's your
guests this time who are busy preparing the pies.

Lost in America

Among the killings. Among the permits. Among the dull transparency. Among the hunger. Among the family beyond my reach. Among the labor pool. Among that type of bread. Among the registered voters, among the paperless statements. Among the eye of the beholder. I'm lost among your ethics. Among New World glossaries. Among the pages of windows. I'm lost inside your mesosphere on what's toxic and what's not—in America. I am certainly lost at the political match. Among recurring wars no one dares to injure on the ride home. Among the ink tracking, MY GOD, new moods helping to reimagine a world beyond the sunrise. Among the maps they used to leave in our hair. "Celia got away, bad hip and all." Among electronic billboards jammed with the Black faces of runaways, don't call this toll-free number if you see her armed and dangerous, healing from the law. Among marijuana fields owned by the same old same old. Against the embargo of time.

People Are Unbearably Docile

after Tim Earley

Smoke the rot, sink the rot, float the rot, listing the rot. Buried in finger
wavy waggy whites and colorstruck veal. Pinching latergrams and
stay rot. Ferry the rot joyfully to a political bed. Mirror the rot pitch
and let everything go. Sluicy patty turntable get down at a schmancy
fancy blight mcdonald's to partake in munchable corporate community
outreach. Punch book of rot songs solid walk of fame shame. Tumble
back the rot in sample lip drip browsers for prez Parasite Mouth gullet
muscle tantrum lantern time. Terrarium the rot in sneaker groom feds
and colonel data farming culottes. Decide on a change of course and
lotus the rot mindfully. Secure rot in molar positivity shrapnelbag.
Handy mandy candy the legal tender collaboration rot. Fairytale
sparkle tooth domestic teething ring rot. Let everything crawl into my
open bone poem robe rot. Sharpen my lunch out of their promissory
notes rot. Don't untie my bib until tomorrow rot. Omfg. Sirloin it.
Alpha cleansing device securing the rot. In a mountain slurry. In a
basic foam hotel. Scion the rot and gargle bleachy clean zoo cab stool.
Carded for buying spraypaint again rot. Duck. Amplify online validity
straw man urgency facing something much worse rot. Flag the rot, boil
the rot, test the rot. For degradation and sway. Slaying staying sold
cold talent wallets rot. Saccharine jolly moomaw east side banner hill
employables rot. Stank wash stinkhorn window. These iconic blitzkrieg
sutures are giving me raw handled life in an enameled hearse rot.
Organ rejection medicine and hasty demographical surgery. Annexed
in my harvest mauled body. Milquetoast midcentury curdled oyster
goblet rot. Aesthete blue prop collars secreting world bank structural
adjustment rot. Uninvited staph foundations mutualizing rot in grand
cerebral chop table theory. Nose the rot. Stuck. Friends fidgeting
from swaddling mushroom bond wand holds. Flung maga wormbags
proverbial snack attack rot. Jfc. What is suitable to wear with imperial
fungus ring around my brimming dump democratic rot. Gunk from

old irons still governing around superlative ankles. Peace signing
your softpedal visionary war gear weapon finger at the high crush
caucus hall rot. Mootsie footsie tootsie the rot. Austere milk pudding
columbus riding crop on display for the hopeful glamcampers pantone
arrowroot rot. Export or perish hamhash malnutrition fugue feels
and electoral ballgown on the patagonia drone committee rot. Double
issue paper trail goober starter pack rot. Armed wagon lyft to the slop
sink brisket bank. Gooey lysol creatives postpore clean teen dream
filling out orders for competitive eagle arms petwork rot. Society is
a fuckcake launch party. No relief hoping on critical mass mutiny
momentum of experimental direct action intervention of a funk punk
black pyromania. Thunderstruck manure shift parching. Give some
illegal gas power rock. Stewing simulacra shook meat. Encouraged by
hivemind repulsion in a trampoline mirror flux. Body microbacterial
compassion rot. Mixing my manic xennial vulnerability with futurism
high and graduation scheme low. Baked out of my ketchup stained
skirt steak mind. Gun solo please rot. Feeling butter mean as hell
today. Deadline it. Front page lookbook eager for a successful
oligarchy thrash down. Let them eat one another. In the meantime
soul tune emptying wounds rescued from the hotbox in a concentric
reciprocal key . . .

Crash Blue Sunday

I don't want to clean but my mind is sick

best thing to do is pick up a broom & forget about it

but I don't want to do what's good for me

I only wanna to do what's good for you

the woman in the mirror is cutting a curse for you

I don't want to change diapers but my heart is sick

best thing to do is change my own & forget about it

but I don't want to do a damn thing that's good for me

I only wanna to do what's good for you

the woman in the mirror is mending a curse for you

I don't want to cook no food but my belly is sick

best thing to do is throw up the poison & forget about it

but I don't want to struggle with feeling well today

I don't wanna to do what's good for you

I'm the woman in the mirror writing a curse on you

I don't want to try today honey

I don't want to feel good

I don't want to forget today baby

I'm not in a forgiving mood

for the people of this world tryin

to pull me down to tell me

it's alright

it's gonna be alright

I'd Come Back from the Grave to Celebrate the End of Capitalism

A sweating flower bed where my fantasies are thinning.
I'm a light sleeper, too many asters, taxonomies of sound.

I'd come in a pair of wide-leg JNCOs like I was meant to be.
Curious, maladaptive, suffused with unrationalized hope.

I'd listen and be with my people. No one is concerned
with honoring success; the concept of success is gone.

In the '90s I knew a scene kid who dreamed about it on
the regular. She had a reputation for going to rave parties

barefoot so she could be close to the rotating basslines,
her body swan diving into the mothership of a 4/4 beat.

Early morning in the trip-hop lounge she once told me
how it was gonna be in the end. We'd stumble blinking

into day and the music would keep going w/o turntables,
mixers, drum machines. Overnight we remade ourselves,

heartbeats of Earth, tricked by business as usual,
restored to our original health. It wouldn't be the

idea where we'd be all one, a cruel monotheism,

hearts got their own tertiary logic, nothing is basic,

but we would all be able to hear it. The beginning

of new connections. Ability to bear music holding

life on this planet. Dead from the last heart attack

of this world, I'm the Black girl dozing with bleary

commuters on the Route 12 bus, on weekends

a fire opal hard at worship in the temple of house.

It's like when an opera singer bangs a high note

and a champagne flute breaks, she explained,

except it would be us, crashing, unconditional,

quaking in real time. The elders have a saying,

the beat goes on: Earth's fracturing livelihoods

resurrected by the rhythms of the night.

Butterfly on a Baby's Head

Maybe it was you

Maybe we're marching to the store

Maybe we're coming back from the ballpark

Maybe we're plump robins shopping in your birdbath

Maybe you're a crest of eggs on a backdoor planet

Maybe after the funeral you became a butterfly on a baby's head

Maybe we yowled and high-fived each other for a job well done

Maybe I helped you sit up when you were finished napping

Maybe I'm a cute Black bug and you're a shack of wings

Maybe we're both babies in booster seats looking at each other

Maybe we're watching lava fissures cleave open in Hawaii

Maybe we're helping children escape battlefields in the South

Maybe the missing children we found are napping in a crest of eggs

Maybe you helped me sit up for the last time before I became a wing

Maybe on a quiet planet a child breathing is called a warm breeze

Maybe you're a retired robin bunching my hair into pigtails

Maybe you prepared me for living on battlefields in the West

Maybe after your funeral we watched the Cubs game

and during the seventh-inning stretch we stood with Harry Caray

Cows in the Morning

I hope cows have dreams
it's not a solidness but
a heaviness when they
stand in the pastures
allowing weight to drip
into the sun-flocked hay
coercion brought us here
but the hills smell good
maybe there's a current
flowing through here to
thumb a cool ride on
dreams I'm preparing
wobbling on my tongue
the farmers finally
letting them walk away
from their sore tits
and the mechanical
suckling humans
the drugs we're on
to prevent days without
maximum proclivity
it's a hot spring morning
the herd takes its time
maintenance of relationships

and empty coffee cups
stretching their necks to
get under the fencing
tasting the free grass
nodding in conversation
with the passerby

Lake Come and Gone

I'm in a kayak watching a man dressed as
Uncle Sam waving around a plastic sword
guiding the pontoon parade across the lake.

It's a tradition to adorn boats with beer slides,
streamers, and women wearing screenprint
T-shirts that say "Lakegirl" in collegiate font.

Despite the last four years of spiraling national
leadership, the vacationers deliver convincing
displays of loyalty not exempt from doubts.

As for me, the other side of the grand show,
I'm trying to balance my life inside the kayak.
It's their Big Day, the birth of a nation in crisis.

Overhead, a bald eagle appears about fifty feet
from our position—symbolic gesture too good,
too perfect to be true—then I see three tiny birds

attacking the eagle, driving it from their nests,
the mild storms sashaying in, delaying fireworks
until everyone is thinking of going home.

Lonely in a Fundamental Way

Little rabbits cooking barbecue in the desert

Little rabbits removing their headwraps for TSA

Little rabbits who prefer modeling in sunglasses

Little rabbits bopping to the store for condoms

Little rabbits smoking Newport Menthol 100s

Little rabbits assembling a brand-new bookshelf

Little rabbits shelling out cash for a wristwatch

Little rabbits shaking out their boots for scorpions

Little rabbits filling out passport applications

Little rabbits who side-eye the moon landing

Little rabbits who appreciate a good utility knife

Little rabbits praying to Black Mary of Częstochowa

Little rabbits tussling with the wrong locker combination

Little rabbits who relax their hair in locked bathrooms

Little rabbits hiking in dormant volcano landscapes

Little rabbits who crack their gum when the bell rings

Little rabbits who snarl back when you least expect it

Further Notes on the New Reconstruction

From the kitchens where the gas is kept,
beloved are the blues shining my shoulder
old potholes knotted by masking the work.
What I need for morning escapes as steam,
night groaning over into a spume of dawn.
To prepare a meal before the next sunrise
means risking everything to write it down.

Down the big halls through rivers & woods
are devils cradled in an old palace of deals.
Windbag so loud a people gets saturated on
while we soothe a bisque of whispers.
Electric stoves won't get the job done but
if that's all you got—we can downlink fire,
like two dense stars shifting the dark fields
confronting desolation 130 billion years ago.

But the recipe (in theory) is pretty simple.
What it takes is a relish for a new undoing—
eventually you'll get what you set out to get.
Stone soup: also known as politicians' wheel,
a hypogeal bone forged by Black Sisypheans
who were smart enough to realize when they

reached the top of their blinking mountain all

they had to do was step aside & the rest

would take care of itself.

Catfish

after Jimi Hendrix

My arms are grown-woman scales
we're swimming for another tide
I got the range of the ancients
we move the mountains around
in the sea and rearrange the new

I'm a saucy fish with a big mouth
when small fry come up watch out
hardheaded women capsize ships
queuing waves, smacking our lips

The deep blue sea is gonna have
to be big enough for you and me
over here now all you waterbabies
taking over swells of groundwater
cracking castles with night swims

Over half the earth is my homeland
we have work to do and I'm thirsty
I got the range of the underseas
we move their stiff cities around
on land and rearrange the old

Just Because We're Scared Doesn't Mean We're Wrong

When language fails me I look around.
Has language failed you, too?
I am a seaworthy underwriter,
chauffeuring the limousine malware.
You're not supposed to put new wine
in old bottles but people do it anyway.
Swelling epochs in shady hunter green,
tragic preoccupations with Hollywood.
I can still pass as a pretty young thing,
take my cue when it's time to butterfly
inside a collapsing salt mine I'm partially
shouldering, shuddering encryptions.
Blink twice if you feel betrayed as I do,
baby, it's whatever I can pull off in a day.

Mosquitoland

What's left behind
is sometimes worse
than the taking

I've gotten over
the ick factor

If flying mamas
need a dab of
blood for eggs

Their lives
short and unfair
go for it

Bite me
you deserve it

Live as long as u can
Idc

The lineage of
a proboscis
soaks the rays

Okay
that's kinda cool
actually

DNA joining all
sorts of creatures
in mothership bods

Traveling through
even larger
cultural bod(ies)

Hey yeah I know
diseases are passed
yes yes I know

It's a drag
how a lack of
imagination
invites tiny welts

I'll scratch you
in a distracted way
and shove off

But like I said

It's a passive act
of sustaining some
kind of life

When the bites
we leave behind

Take 1000+ years
to dismantle

All Dogs Go to Heaven

Beloved, we call you brave
hoping the bare limit
for human reign is terminal,
your rehabilitation to be
dangerously free. Inside
your paws longings twinge
while you sleep. I awake
because you are newborn,
a terrifying responsibility
I'll be human to you, lead
you on a leash, hate myself
for it, holler when you run
down the road when I let
you go. The truth is I love
watching you trot away
from me: you look like
yourself, whoever that is,
natural dog engaging in
an unnatural world making
stops to rebury your bones,
doing what dogs are allowed
to do, without me.

Black Woman in a Bathtub, Twenty-First Century

I am a hippopotamus woman
who's got a date with Dr. Teal.
Cedar and eucalyptus guiding
the banks of my plastic tub river.

I sink and let fly a delicious hum.
Open my mouth to call butterflies.
Birds use my back as a notepad,
the children are shopping in town.

I am a woman alone in a house.
Bubbles and mud salve my legs.
Downwind I hear the hippo boys,
but it's got nothing to do with me.

I am a happy woman in her bath.
I am the babysitter of all yr rivers.
I'll be here long after you're gone,
I'll be here when it's time to return.

Anti-Elegy

Honey, my earth is merciful. You understand?
I call you mine not as ownership but because
you are a part of me. I pick up pine needles by
the lake, the bright smell coaxing me out of my
estrangement from life and back into it again.
There are lily pads of ice on the surface so we
throw stones to gain an advantage—but it's still
too close, still too new. A bird's feather declines
to weigh in on my basic jealousies w/ the body
it came from, far beyond our sightseeing skills.
When a rock you chucked pauses on the ice
I consider whether I'm capable, the responsibility
of being a decisive witness—to labor from land

to tributary in a season. Then it shows up as
soft spots crumbling out of the tangy ledges
at our feet, like my hair falling out in the shower.
I don't have enough time to loosen the space
handing out more than I can renew. Water is
brittle and endorses rude dictionaries of what
folks looked like the last time you saw them,
and every year there are odd thunderstorms
in December when the snow should be cooling

out on big summers w/ the longest trespasses.

This particular frost props up the top of a lie, but

you're in another garden now that only looks

like you when the light shifts.

Take a Seat

Adirondack, folding, lawn, barstool,
recliner, beanbag, swivel, car seat,

egg, bleacher, ergonomic, windsor,
vanity, saddle, computer, lazy boy,

chaise longue, pilgrim, potty, elbow,
fiddleback, shaker, director's, bubble,

sling, wicker, chippendale, sedan,
hassock, camp, kneeling, rocking,

banker, bistro, renaissance, goth,
gravity, sleeping-bag, military, high,

barcelona, knotted, inflatable, lawn,
revolving, wingback, cradle, throne

Lullaby

Sleep like their terrible gods have left you

and obscurity is a passive worry again,

creatures who prefer my dark to the light.

No investments in the temples of time,

no bubbling oversights or official portraits.

All that has clicked to your hammer today,

all that has finished you off as a rosy spectator,

your job, your birdcage, opens onto a bridge

exhaled by the rain of the get-gone.

The golden blood you've fancied at work

is cutting off another rare circulation.

I reach over and dial down your tempo.

You don't want to play that song over here.

You've been unconscious all day, sweetie,

and now you need some rest.

Birthday

Picked some wildflowers,
what was left. Head-tossing
leaves and primordial guides,
new shoots growing off a ripe
mother leaf in cantaloupe hollow.
One of your best sentences today
was when I asked where you were,
"I'm by this tree Mama!" Playing with
gravel and crust so you ran, laughed,
made me search for your little cars that
you tossed into a union of stinging nettles.
I was born today and I'm not that bad at this
parenthood thing in a sweated-up lounge dress,
slip-on sandals and competent headscarf following
you instead of taking a shower or watching my shows,
guiding you back to the house so I can place the later
blossoms in water, change your pants first since you have
burrs all over your backside, preheat the oven for chicken,
scold the dog for not cooling his strength when he plays with you.
It's not the ideal flower arrangement. But why should it have to be.

Ars Poetica on a Twenty-Dollar Bill

When I'm dead
I won't know this life

If I keep working
past my death
that's on the living

If the living don't care
how I worked for them
while I was alive

know that I died

as a Black woman
who lived in America
and I survived

well versed

on what

the living dead were

inspired by

Mother of Thousands

Bryophyllum daigremontianum, commonly called mother of thousands, alligator plant, or Mexican hat plant, is a succulent plant native to Madagascar.

Underneath the fields is where our stories are buried. The monocrops were decisions made about our past, so I ask you to take the batteries out of the clanging wall clock before I go to sleep to prevent the supremacist art of domestication from permeating my dreams.

Inside my raised fist is a struggling livelihood: sugarcane, corn & certainly cotton. I've come here to climb the spiral rope back to the knowledge of the land, holding a scythe branded with the name I gave myself & my hands ache so much from having to dig you out,

I stop at every county cemetery no matter who is resting there. I am a gatherer of thousands, how you said we don't have to buy seeds driving past a town named Coon Valley as I inwardly flinched about a strange joke E. used to make about not seeing a relative "in a coon's age,"

& the day I realized what she meant by that when she said it, how my fist in the will of my stomach began to wilt, their freshly mowed lawns burning with the crosses of their wickedness. A mother ushering her children to safety, a story carried on by the next generation of plantlets,

since water has been proved to secure history, when public wailing feels like you're a conduit for someone else. Caring for an unmarked grave on her lunch hour, autocratic fields you can see from an airplane window seat. We touch our callused feet together. Underneath this land is a

succulent downpour we are building from the lives calling to be excavated. The fists of Black & Brown women throughout the ages in a controlled heirloom heat. Seeds taking flight from the ancient fields of our wildflower palms for we are the mothers of thousands.

About the Author

Nikki Wallschlaeger is a Black poet who currently lives in the Driftless region of Wisconsin, enjoying country life and its many strange synchronicities and surprises. You can find her on Twitter @nikkimwalls where she welcomes respectful conversation and correspondence. This is her third book.

Poetry is vital to language and living. Since 1972, Copper Canyon Press has published extraordinary poetry from around the world to engage the imaginations and intellects of readers, writers, booksellers, librarians, teachers, students, and donors.

WE ARE GRATEFUL FOR THE MAJOR SUPPORT PROVIDED BY:

THE PAUL G. ALLEN
FAMILY FOUNDATION

CULTURE

Lannan

ART WORKS.

National
Endowment
for the Arts
arts.gov

OFFICE OF ARTS & CULTURE
SEATTLE

WASHINGTON STATE
ARTS COMMISSION

TO LEARN MORE ABOUT UNDERWRITING
COPPER CANYON PRESS TITLES,
PLEASE CALL 360-385-4925 EXT. 103

WE ARE GRATEFUL FOR THE MAJOR SUPPORT PROVIDED BY:

Anonymous

Jill Baker and Jeffrey Bishop

Anne and Geoffrey Barker

In honor of Ida Bauer, Betsy
Gifford, and Beverly Sachar

Donna and Matthew Bellew

Will Blythe

John Branch

Diana Broze

John R. Cahill

Sarah Cavanaugh

The Beatrice R. and Joseph A.
Coleman Foundation

The Currie Family Fund

Laurie and Oskar Eustis

Austin Evans

Saramel Evans

Mimi Gardner Gates

Gull Industries Inc. on behalf of
William True

The Trust of Warren A. Gummow

Carolyn and Robert Hedin

William R. Hearst, III

Bruce Kahn

Phil Kovacevich and Eric Wechsler

Lakeside Industries Inc. on behalf
of Jeanne Marie Lee

Maureen Lee and Mark Busto

Peter Lewis and Johnna Turiano

Ellie Mathews and Carl Youngmann
as The North Press

Larry Mawby and Lois Bahle

Hank and Liesel Meijer

Jack Nicholson

Gregg Orr

Petunia Charitable Fund and
adviser Elizabeth Hebert

Gay Phinny

Suzanne Rapp and Mark Hamilton

Adam and Lynn Rauch

Emily and Dan Raymond

Jill and Bill Ruckelshaus

Cynthia Sears

Kim and Jeff Seely

Stephanie Ellis-Smith and Douglas
Smith

Joan F. Woods

Barbara and Charles Wright

Caleb Young as C. Young Creative

The dedicated interns and
faithful volunteers of
Copper Canyon Press

The Chinese character for poetry is made up of two parts:
"word" and "temple." It also serves as pressmark for
Copper Canyon Press.

The poems are set in Sabon.
Book design and composition by Phil Kovacevich.